D1563306

Addicted: A Bad Boy Stepbrother Romance

By Lauren Landish

"Your lips would look great wrapped around my..."

Who in the world tells a girl that on their first meeting? Tyler Locklin, that's who. He's filthy rich and arrogant with a set of abs that is the envy of all young men everywhere, and did I forget to mention devilishly handsome? He's a bastard of the first order. I can't stand to be in the same room with him.

But with one wink or a flash of his mischievous grin, I go weak in the knees. It pisses me off. I'm supposed to hate him. He's an asshole. Yet, I can't help but be drawn to him because I'm . . .
ADDICTED.

**Full-length novel with an HEA, no cheating, and no cliffhanger!

Table of Contents

Prologue

Victoria

I squirmed beneath the silken sheets, the last vestiges of an earth-shattering orgasm coursing through my sweat-covered limbs. My breasts rose and fell below the sheets as I tried to catch my breath and regain control. After a while, my racing pulse slowly started to calm down as the tremors slowly receded. At last, a sigh escaped my lips as my body was flooded by a rush of hormones.

It was always this way.

He takes me, ravaging my body for everything that it's worth . . . and then leaves. It's a game he plays. He wants to leave me in a state of desperation, aching for more of his touch. Aching to feel his lips all over my body. He leaves, knowing that I'll still be there when he comes back, wanting every piece of him.

Bastard.

I should've left him. I had every right to. But whenever I think I've finally had enough, I make up reasons why I can't. Maybe it's because he's one of the richest men in the country.

Maybe it's that incredible swagger or that cocky grin that says he can fuck any woman he wants. Or maybe it's because I like feeling his eight-inch cock plowing through me like no tomorrow.

The truth is, being with him is a huge ego boost for a girl like me. He's handsome, powerful and mysterious, and I'm a small town girl with dreams of becoming big in the fashion world. Being with him is downright intoxicating. Addicting. And I can never get enough.

There's just one problem . . . he's my stepbrother.

Chapter 1
Victoria

A fool. That's what my mother has always called me for choosing a career in the fashion industry. Why can't I aspire to work in a real industry with more stability? She'd ask.

"Because that's always been my dream, Mother," I'd say.

"Well, sorry to tell you, sweetheart, but dreams don't pay the bills."

Then she'd go on to berate me, telling me how much of a mistake I was making with my life. It got so bad that after I graduated from college and got a job as a personal assistant for one of the most popular designers in the city, Christine Finnerman, we had a huge falling out. I don't know what it was with her and my pursuing my dream of fashion.

Every day, she would call me to tell me that
late to turn around and do something else with my l
would offer alternatives to my career choice—all of
hated with a passion. For a while I put up with her nc
suggestions, but I was infuriated every second that I h.
to her complaining, and it took great effort to hold it a
mean, isn't it a parent's duty to encourage their child's h
dreams and aspirations? Not so for my mother. She seer
take a special kind of glee in telling me I was doing it all

Finally, I could take no more. The feelings that I'd
holding back had boiled over and I soon started getting int
shouting matches with my mother, saying things better left
unsaid. Of course, none of these arguments ever ended well
we ended up not speaking to each other for weeks at a time.

It was so bad that when her wedding came about, I di
go. She was marrying some filthy rich guy that she'd callously
divorced my father for.

I figured if she thought I was such a failure, then she
wouldn't want me showing up at her wedding, embarrassing her
in front of her high-class guests.

In truth, I also didn't go because I was still angry about
the divorce. My mother had up and left my dad without so much
as an explanation, simply stating that she wasn't happy in her
marriage and hadn't been for a very long time. I thought it had
more to do with the new man she was seeing, who had a far, far
larger bank account.

After all, my mom has always had a taste for the finer
things in life, you understand.

It didn't seem to hurt my father, however, since he had a

new girlfriend half his age within a week of the divorce. My father, it seemed, had already been dipping his toes in the younger pool way before things turned south in his marriage. Perhaps it was the real reason why Mother left him. Whatever the case, despite being angry about the divorce, I didn't approve of my father's behavior either. The girl he was with was around my age and dumb as a sack of potatoes. To make matters worse, he had plans to marry her and start a family. Out of distaste, I started shunning my father's company as well, because when it came down to it, I couldn't tolerate a girl that was basically the same age as me being my stepmother.

So here I am, in a big city, parentless, with only my dreams and aspirations to guide me.

* * *

A sharp voice snapped me to attention.

"Where is my coffee?"

I froze, a stack of papers filled with clothing designs, measurements and fashion models bundled in my arms. Slowly, I turned around to see Christine Finnerman, my boss, leaning against her desk, her palm resting against the polished wood. She impatiently tapped on her desk with her immaculate nails, making a clack, clack, clack sound.

As usual, she was dressed as sharp as a tack. A white dress wrapped around her matronly frame, fitting her like a glove, and a shiny black belt circled her waist, giving her shapely figure a va-voom appearance. She was wearing black glossy heels I'd contemplate killing my mother for, and not one bit of her shoulder-length hair, which is a striking pepper gray, was out of place.

"I'm sorry, Christine," I said when I could finally manage, trying to push down the anxiety that was suddenly rushing up my throat. "I was just about to get it. I didn't expect you to arrive ten minutes early."

Christine eyed me with contempt reserved for a dog. "One should always be prepared for the unexpected, especially in this industry." She paused for dramatic effect. *Hurry up.* I swear she spoke the last words with her mouth closed.

"Right away."

Scrambling in my three-inch Christian Dior heels—a job perk that I particularly enjoyed—I made my way to my desk that's in the adjoining room to Christine's office. I threw the stack down on it, breathing in and out, trying to catch my breath. I was wearing a tight black dress that makes it difficult for me to breathe as well as move because it's a size too small. Christine told me that at a size eight, I'm fat by industry standards, so I'd started trying to squeeze into smaller dress sizes, hoping that the discomfort would encourage me to lose weight.

Once I thought I could breathe again, I scurried over to the professional Keurig machine that sat in the hallway leading up to Christine's office. A few seconds later, I'm setting down a steaming mug on her desk.

I stepped back and beamed proudly as if I'd just won a nationwide competition. "Will that be all?" I asked her, my tone respectful.

Christine didn't even bother to look up at me as she flipped through the pages of a fashion book. "You may go," she said, motioning her hands as if she was shooing a fly.

I turned away, feeling dejected. I hated how Christine

treated me, but I was used to it. I saw my tenure as her indentured slave as a necessary sacrifice. As one of the most powerful women in the fashion world, working for Christine would open up many doors for me.

And once that door opens, I'm going to run through it, slam it, and never look back.

I made it to the door before Christine spoke again. "Oh, and Victoria, I need you to call Adam Pierre to tell him I won't be attending his show next week."

I turned back around, my mouth agape like a frog. "But . . . Adam throws one of the biggest shows in the industry," I dared to protest. "You can't just not show up."

Christine looked up from her book, her expression sharp enough to cut glass.

It was the only answer I needed.

"I'll get right on it," I squeaked.

I scurried back to my desk and flopped down in my seat. Blowing strands of hair out of my eyes in frustration, I took a deep breath and picked up the phone. Did I mention that I really hated working for Christine? I consider myself a pretty headstrong girl who can speak up for myself whenever I feel like I'm being mistreated, but in the face of Christine Finnerman's wrath, I became a doormat—mainly because I so desperately needed my job.

I quickly dialed Pierre's number.

"Bonjour?"

I was surprised when Pierre himself answered. Usually he had some lackey to handle his affairs, but when Christine Finnerman was calling, I guess even if you're the busiest honcho in town, you have time.

"Mr. Pierre?" I asked nervously. "This is Victoria Young, Christine Finnerman's assistant."

"Ah yes, Victoria," Pierre said in his heavy French accent. "Christy has told me a lot about you."

None of it good, I'm sure.

Sweat beaded my palms. "I'm sorry to tell you this, sir, but Christine has informed me that she must cancel for your upcoming show."

Pierre let out a gasp, sounding like he was choking on a hot dog. "What? Impossible! If she doesn't show up, it'll be a disaster." I could hear frantic movement through the phone and a rustling of papers. "Where is Christine?" he demanded a moment later. "I must speak to her."

I glanced up from my desk. Christine had made it absolutely clear that she wanted to cancel. If I went inside of her office and tried to convince her otherwise, I might be out of a job. She doesn't have patience for employees questioning her decisions.

"I am very sorry, Pierre," I insisted, "but Christine must respectfully decline. Perhaps I can call around for a replacement for you?" Of course I'm just blowing hot air. As one of the biggest names in the fashion world, one couldn't simply replace Christine Finnerman.

Pierre's breathing was erratic. "What will it take?" he rasps. "What will it take for Christine to show up?" The sounds of tears in his voice tugged at my heart strings. "My reputation is riding on this."

I took a deep breath, feeling bad for the man. But what

could I do for him?

"Please, Victoria," he begged me. "Get her to speak with me."

It wasn't lost on me that here was a powerful man himself, begging me to get my boss to listen to him.

And that's why I'm working for her. Because in the eyes of the fashion world, Christine Finnerman is God.

I sat there listening to Pierre's pathetic begging, not sure what to do. Finally, I could take no more. "Hold on," I told him. I got up from my desk and took the phone with me.

I made it to Christine's office doorway when the telephone line went taut. I couldn't move any further. Normally I'd have just put him on hold. I don't know what had come over me.

What am I doing?

I placed the phone against my hip to block out sound.

"Christine?" I dared.

She looked up at me and my heart jumped in my chest. "What is it, Victoria? Have you told Pierre that I'm not coming?"

"Uh," I mumbled. Then I took a deep breath and gathered my courage. "I'm sorry, Christine, but he's adamant that he speaks with you—"

"Since when does telling a client that I will not be attending mean that you must listen to his pathetic whining and feel honor-bound to go against my orders, hmm?"

Blood rushed to my cheeks as I fumbled for an answer.

"But," Christine continued, "Since you're fairly new here and quite easy to influence, I'll forgive you—just this once." She sat back in her seat and appraised me with her frost-blue eyes.

"Now tell me, what does Mr. Pierre want?"

I pushed down the anger that rose in my throat at her insult. "He wants to know what it will take for you to attend."

Christine stared at me for a long moment. "There is a designer by the name of Amanda Kersey. Heard of her? Terrible designer with clothing that looks like a blind woman designed it and models that look like they're meth addicts straight off the streets. Anyway, a trusted advisor told me she used choice words in speaking about me . . ."

Christine's words trailed off, but her meaning was clear. She gave me a direct look to drive her point home, and I shook involuntarily at what she wanted me to do. Much like me, Amanda Kersey is young and starry-eyed. She's a popular upcoming designer, who I'm sure has a lot riding on this.

And with one word, Christine destroys her.

My immediate urge was to hang up the phone, tell Christine to kiss my ass, and then walk out of her office for good. But as a newly-graduated twenty-two-year-old who was estranged from both parents and alone in a big city with a lease to pay, I couldn't afford to piss off such a powerful woman.

"Is there a problem?" Christine asked me.

Numbly, I shook my head and raised the phone to my lips.

"Pierre?" I ask weakly.

He was still there after all this time.

"Yes?"

Despite the grave situation, I almost laughed at the desperation in his voice.

"There is a fashion designer by the name of Amanda

Kersey—"

"She's done," Pierre cut in. "I'll be calling her immediately to tell her that something came up and someone else will be taking her place."

The line went dead and I stood there, feeling numb all over.

"Victoria?" Christine said to me. I looked over at her, noting the wicked curl to her lips. She'd won her little power play and now could privately gloat. "Stop standing there like an imbecile and get to work."

She's really testing me.

Holding back an acidic reply, I turned away and numbly walked back to my desk, slamming the phone down. I grasped my head in my palms and blew out a stressful breath. After a moment, I straightened up and began going through Christine's schedule, marking the calendar for Pierre's show.

As much as I wanted to quit my job, I knew if I stuck it out for a little while longer, big things would happen for me. At least that's what I hoped.

"That door just can't open quick enough," I muttered to myself.

Chapter 2
Tyler

"You've got to get your shit together, man," Jeff growled at me.

Sitting back in my chair, I winced as a sharp pain sliced through my brain. As usual, I'd stayed up late after a night of drinking and wild sex. It would've been worth it, but the girl I'd gone home with last night, a blonde with big tits and a nice round ass, had been too eager to suck my dick.

I like a challenge, a girl who likes to play hard to get, and lately, all of them have given it up without any effort from me.

Too easy.

It probably had something to do with the fact that I was a man of wealth, co-founder of Armex Corp with my father, James Locklin. Or maybe it was just my confident swagger. I was, after all, six-foot-three, tall, blonde and cut like exquisitely carved stone thanks to my workout regimen.

Jeff hissed with exasperation and leaned across the table. "Are you listening to me?"

The pain in my skull pounded relentlessly. I didn't want to listen to this shit. How many times had I heard it before? Ten? Twenty? A hundred? Who gives a fuck? I don't.

"You can't keep sleeping around with these groupie sluts," Jeff continued. "As one of the top executives, you're making Armex look bad."

I settled my gaze on Jeff. With dark brown hair and hazel eyes, he was a few years my senior. He was dressed in a business suit that made him look older than what he really was. I think he needed to lighten up and go out and get some pussy, then maybe he wouldn't be so uptight all the time. I could fix him up in one night.

"I don't see how the girls I fuck are any business of the company," I responded in a cavalier tone that I knew would piss Jeff off. I enjoyed getting under people's skin, for no other reason than I knew I could without consequence.

It worked.

"Well, it is when it's affecting our public image and our bottom line," Jeff growled back at me, his face twisting into an angry scowl. "If you made sure no one saw you publicly consorting with those skanks, then it would be different. Since you don't, the board members are getting tired of it. They're tired of your making us look unprofessional."

Anger boiled up from my rock-hard abs. How dare my peers complain about my private business? I was the co-founder of the fucking company. They wouldn't be shit without me.

"That's bullshit, Jeff, and you know it. Since when is it a crime to have a life outside of your place of business? Shit, half these guys cheat on their wives behind their backs and have the fucking nerve to tell me that I can't live the way I want to on my own time? Fuck off."

I didn't miss the poorly-hidden smile flash across Jeff's face. "All I know is, if you don't start behaving soon, you might be out of a job. There's talk of a vote. Co-founder or not . . ."

Enraged, I jumped out of my chair and regretted it a

second later. The pain stabbed my brain like a hammer pounding a nail into wood. "A vote?" I snorted, fighting back the momentary dizziness that overcame me. "The fuck for? Are they going to demote me? Fire me? They can't do that. My dad will—"

Jeff gave me his infamous *gotcha* smirk. "Your dad is in agreement."

I froze momentarily, shocked. I couldn't believe that my dad, the biggest womanizer I know, could be party to something as asinine as this.

"Your dad thinks if you're to become CEO one day, you have to drop the bad boy image. Instead of rolling around with the local sluts, maybe it's time you start looking for a suitable partner. Settle down."

"Fuck that." The idea appalled me. I'd been in a serious relationship before and it didn't turn out well. I'd worn my heart on my sleeve only to get fucked royally in the end when I caught her cheating on me. On *me*.

After that, I'd decided that no girl was worthy of my love, and my new motto was to fuck 'em and then leave 'em.

Jeff stared at me. "This isn't a game, Tyler. You need to seriously get it together or face losing your position in the company." He paused, smirking once again. "Charles Whitmore is looking to take your spot if you don't shape up."

I stared at him incredulously. "Is this a fucking joke?" It had to be. I couldn't imagine my father listening to such bullshit. Charles Whitmore, my nemesis at Armex, had swiftly risen through the ranks of the corporate world. Although pretty douche, he was only a few years older and a pretty shrewd businessman—as much as I hated to admit it.

Still, there was no way he could fill my shoes. No fucking way. This had to be one huge conspiracy by my lesser peers to fuck with me.

Jeff shook his head. "Nope. Not at all."

"I don't believe this," I growled. "I'm going to talk to my father about it. I don't believe for one second that he'd ever go against me."

Jeff leaned back in his chair and continued to grin at me, making me want to smash his face in. "You do that."

* * *

"You have become a liability to the company," my father said to me. I was standing at his desk in his swanky office within his three-story mansion, and I needed a strong drink to take in what I was hearing.

I studied him with disbelief. My father's a big man, barrel-chested with greying hair, and a complete egomaniac. He was dressed in a business suit, his tie loosened and his blazer draped over the back of his chair.

I thought Jeff was blowing hot air when he told me that my father was in compliance with this nonsense. To hear it from the horse's mouth enraged me.

"Word of your . . ." my father paused, searching for the right word to describe my antics that had riled everyone up, "*play* has gotten around and is traveling around the corporate circles."

I began to protest, but my father raised a stern finger to quiet me. "Ordinarily your behavior wouldn't be a problem. You're a grown man who's free to do whatever you choose when it comes to your personal life. But, a large demographic of

18

Armex customers hold family values in high regard. If you continue to . . . misbehave in public, then the board will vote to replace you."

I couldn't believe what I was hearing.

"I founded this fucking company with you," I growled as I stabbed a finger at the ground, anger burning my throat. "You can't replace me."

My dad stared at me calmly. "Yes, you did. And despite your bad habits that you've developed over the years, you are a wonderful businessman—shrewd as they come. But in order for our company to survive, concessions must be made. Clean up your act—or else."

"Are you fucking serious?" I shouted, unable to control my anger any longer.

He didn't answer, but he didn't have to. He was dead serious. He wanted to out me. His son. Me, who'd helped him build the company from the ground up. And for what? All because I scorned relationships and liked to get pussy whenever and however I wanted?

"Listen to yourself!" I continued. "If you had any balls, you would tell them to go fuck themselves. I'm your son, for Christ's sake! Armex wouldn't be shit without me."

His jaw bulged and he gripped the edge of his desk, a sign that my words had gotten to him.

"Charles Whitmore?" I demanded. "Charles fucking Whitmore?"

"He's shown himself to be an exemplary employee, and he wants to see this company to the next level . . ."

Unlike you.

His words trailed off, but I heard the unspoken meaning behind them.

Clearing his throat, Dad stood up and grabbed his coat from the back of his chair. "I'm sorry that you're angry, son. But this really shouldn't be a problem. The solution is simple. Stop with the public womanizing and keep your job."

"You let those assholes vote against me, and I'll make sure you regret it." The words left my lips before I could stop them.

He paused for a moment, considering my words. Finally, he said, "Choose your battles carefully, son." He shrugged on his coat. "I'm going to pick up Martha from the Bolingers'. They're planning a dinner party for an event later this month. If you haven't dug yourself into a hole by then, I expect you to attend." He walked from the room, leaving me standing there simmering with anger.

Martha was his newlywed wife. I'd only met her twice, once at the wedding and another time at a family function. She was nice enough, I guess, but a woman who had no real assets to speak of. It was a mystery why my dad chose to marry her.

"Oh, trust me, Dad," I said to myself as I walked over to the cabinet behind his desk and pulled out a bottle of brandy along with a glass. I needed something to drink to calm the frustration that I felt. "I have every intention of fighting this battle."

Chapter 3
Tyler

"Your life is over," I said, smacking down a glass on the bar counter.

Brad, my childhood best friend, peered over at me, his eyes bloodshot. He was dressed casually in blue jeans and a black t-shirt, while I was still dressed in my work clothes, black silk slacks and a white dress shirt. I usually dressed well when I went to clubs, flaunting the fact that I had money. "Why do you say that?

We were sitting in a popular bar, you know, one of the trash dens that the company doesn't want to see me in. After my explosive blowout with Dad, Brad called me, saying that he was having relationship problems in the form of his fiancée practically forcing him to give her an official wedding date. To make matters worse, the wedding she wanted was going to cost a fortune and would temporarily bankrupt him.

I'd told Brad that I would meet him and we could both talk about our problems.

"If she's already calling the shots now," I told him, "then what do you think it's going to be like when you're married?"

Brad let out a groan and stared down into his glass with a forlorn expression. "Don't remind me, man. I'm already fucking stressed the hell out. I've only been working at the law firm for less than a year. How the fuck does she expect me to afford the kind of wedding that she wants?"

"What does she want?"

Brad made a sour face. "Everything. I mean, like, her family is huge. She has like ten sisters who must have a hundred little girls, and she wants every last one to be flower girls. She wants to rent out the Promade and have the wedding out on the lawn, complete with an orchestra, band and entertainment. Not to mention, she wants me to provide the clothing for all her immediate family."

I let out a low whistle.

"Tell me about it," Brad continued. "I don't know how Katie thinks we can afford it. I know I have a pretty good job, but damn, at least give on something. If it wasn't for all our student loan debt, we could probably swing it."

I signaled the bartender for another drink—a slender girl dressed in a cut-off top that bared her midriff. She smiled at me and scurried off to the mixer. She wanted my dick, I was sure of it, but I wasn't interested. I usually didn't go for girls who had tattoos, even though I had a couple myself. It was just one of my hypocrisies.

"Where does Katie work again?"

"She's a groomer. She loves animals." Brad laughed. "Hell, I wouldn't be surprised if she'd want me to dress the damn dogs in tuxes too."

"I feel your pain, brother," I said. I really didn't. Brad, I think, had fallen into a trap. After my one true relationship had failed, I'd lost belief in true love. Brad would wind up regretting getting married and getting stuck with kids, mark my words.

Of course, I didn't want to tell him what I really felt,

because I thought it would only piss him off. He had too much invested in this Katie chick at this point, and I've learned it's better to let people make their own mistakes rather than try to dissuade them.

The bartender chick walked over and placed my drink down before me. I reached into my pocket to pay for it when she stopped me.

"It's on the house, handsome," she purred at me with a wink and strutted away to serve some other drunk patron.

Brad shook his head and eyed me with disbelief. "Un-fucking believable. She all but bent over and asked you to fuck her."

"I'm glad she didn't," I said, grabbing the drink and turning it up. "She's not my type."

Brad stared at me. "You're an asshole, you know that?"

I didn't respond. Instead, I roved my eyes over the crowded bar. I saw plenty of girls, all dressed up with tons of makeup, and a few in fuck-me pumps, but none that interested me.

"So what's up with you?" Brad asked, making me turn my attention back to him. "I've never seen you turn up so many so quickly before. What's got you so bent outta' shape?"

"My dad's thinking about replacing me at the company."

Brad's jaw dropped. "You're shitting me."

I shook my head and proceeded to tell Brad everything. "They said I need to stop frequenting clubs, present one included, and picking up random chicks," I said as I got to the end of my tale. "And I should focus on cleaning up my image."

"I don't know, man. Maybe they're right," Brad said after

a moment of thought. I should have known better than to try to get sympathy from him. "A man in your position should be held to a higher standard. Fucking a new slut every weekend doesn't exactly scream professionalism."

"That's the thing," I said. "What I do on my own time is none of anyone else's business."

"True," Brad agreed. "But it is when it affects the business's image. I don't know how you can't see that. I mean, get a grip already, Tyler. You're not fucking nineteen anymore. You should be thinking about settling down and starting a family in a couple of years."

I swallowed back my anger. Brad should've had my back, but deep down, I knew he was right. "That will never happen. The family part, that is. And there's no way I'm going to stop fucking who I want, when I want."

Brad shook his head at me.

"In fact, just out of spite, I'm going to continue to do what I've been doing. Let them come for me. Fuck 'em."

"Seriously?"

"I just need you to represent me when they do." I rolled my shoulders. "Things are about to get ugly."

Brad went slack-jawed. "You want me to represent you against Armex?"

"Yeah. I'm going to call my dad's bluff. There's no fucking way I'm going to let him replace me without a fight. If the board votes on me, I'm going to sue their fucking pants off to take my half of the company."

I gave Brad a direct look. "And I'm going to need your help when I do." Truthfully, Brad was a newbie lawyer and

24

didn't have much experience under his belt, but he was absolutely brilliant, and I knew he'd fight for me harder than anyone else. If I was going to go toe-to-toe with my father, I wanted him on my side.

Brad stared at me a long time before letting out an explosive breath. "Alright, man," he said finally, "but I want to make sure you know what you're getting yourself into if it comes down to that."

"Of course." I smiled at him and clasped his shoulder. "I knew you'd have my back."

Brad still looked sour. "It's just one more stressful situation to add on top of this God damn wedding."

"Let me handle it," I offered suddenly. Brad had agreed to represent me, which was no small thing, since Armex was armed to the teeth with high-powered lawyers. I wanted to reward his loyalty.

Brad immediately held his hands up in protest. "C'mon, man, you don't have to do that."

"It's no problem," I insisted. "In fact, my position at the company affords me a lot of connections. I can get a designer to handle everything. Katie will love it."

Brad was in awe. "You'd do that?"

"Hell yeah, man. It's supposed to be the most special moment of your life. You deserve it."

Brad would never admit it, but I think he was getting slightly emotional on me because his eyes became watery. "Thanks, man, I don't know how I'll ever repay you."

I casually signaled the girl for another drink, and she practically abandoned a patron mid-order in her haste to serve me.

As I watched her sashay over to the mixer, I thought, *maybe it's time to try something new.*

She was over with my drink in a few seconds, setting it down before me. I gave her *the look*. The look I gave to all the girls before I'm ready to fuck them, and her body trembled slightly.

I threw back my drink and replied to Brad, "Don't' sweat it."

Chapter 4
Victoria

"I have a client that needs a wedding gown designed," Christine said to me as I sat down her steaming mug of coffee on her desk. She was nosing through the latest catalogue. "He also needs fittings and measurements for about one hundred wedding guests."

That sounds like an awful amount of work.

I stepped back and folded my hands before me respectfully. "What client is this?" Steam from the coffee reached my nostrils and I felt slightly nauseated. I'd made coffee so much for Christine that I'd come to hate the smell of it.

I thought to myself, *or maybe it's just her that I can't stand.*

Christine glanced up at me as if annoyed by my daring to ask a question. "A young man by the name of Tyler Locklin, co-founder of a company called Armex. From what I hear, he's quite a scoundrel. And if the rumors are true, he'll be out of a job soon." Christine glanced down into her coffee. "However, that won't stop me from working with him. I happen to know his father, James, a very cold, calculating man with deep pockets. His son will be paying dearly for my talents."

I'd never heard of this guy, his father, or their company, and I was surprised Christine kept up with gossip outside of fashion. After all, she lived and breathed it. "Will I be working with him?" I ask.

Christine stared at me for a moment with surprise, and then burst out laughing in a way that made me clench my teeth together. "Oh no, you silly little girl. You'll be helping a small army of fitters and designers get the measurements right for the wedding guests. I've already called and have April and Gabe assembling the team. You'll go along and do everything April tells you to since . . ." Christine paused to look my red dress up and down critically. "she actually has fashion sense."

I clenched my fists. Christine really rubbed me the wrong way. Every day.

Just a little while longer, I told myself. *And that door is going to open up.*

"When do we start?"

Christine picked up her coffee and took a sip before replying. "Today."

* * *

"Holy shit," April swore as we stood outside the back of Finnerman's headquarters, a large corporate building in the middle of downtown. "This is going to be a nightmare."

Despite Christine's annoying penchant for comparing me to her, I liked April. Unlike Christine, she was surprisingly level-headed and treated people like human beings. As Christine's head assistant, she was in charge of the more labor-intensive duties like the one we were about to embark on.

"No shit," Gabe, April's assistant, said. Isn't that funny? Even the head assistant to Christine has an assistant. Blonde, good-looking and armed with dimples, Gabe happened to be gay, which I'm sure had given more than a few girls heartache over his lifetime. He was dressed in simple jeans, dress shirt and a tie, his blonde hair gelled and spiky.

April shook her head. "I don't know what the hell she was thinking when she took on this client. We'll be swamped for days." April turned to me, biting her lower lip. "Vicky, I'm going to need more help from you than usual."

I eyed her with apprehension. "What kind of help?"

"Help keep track of the measurements, who's been fitted, all that kind of stuff."

"And who's the hottest guy packing the most heat," Gabe added in, brandishing a twelve-inch ruler that he randomly pulled out of his pocket. "After all, aren't we going there to do measurements?"

April and I cracked up and Gabe winked at us mischievously.

"So can I count on you?" April asked when we stopped laughing.

I sobered quickly. Despite knowing that I wouldn't be mistreated by April, somehow I knew this undertaking was going to leave me exhausted, overworked and under-appreciated. But what other choice did I have?

"Of course," I replied.

Chapter 5
Tyler

"I'll be along to help you in just a minute, Mr. Locklin," said a girl who introduced herself as April. She was obviously in charge of the fitting operation. She was a small, mousey thing.

She was dressed in a flowing, flowery dress that reminded me of summer, her hair pulled back into a business-like ponytail. She was cute, in a wholesome, girl next door way, but she wasn't my type.

Usually, if I can't imagine a girl's lips wrapped around my dick, I know she's not for me.

Crossing my arms across my chest, I casually leaned against a column in the large reception hall with private dressing rooms I'd rented out for Brad's wedding and for him and his fiancée's family to use for the fittings. Both families would be stopping in and out all day to get measurements. "No problem," I told her. "Take your time."

She beamed at me for a moment before leaving off, shouting orders. I watched her in boredom, my thoughts wandering.

This is all so unnecessary, I thought to myself as I stared at all the hubbub of activity.

The sad thing is, what Katie wanted cost a fortune, even without hiring a top designer to design it all. Luckily for Brad, I was footing the bill. For me it was just a drop in the bucket. It was the least I could do.

Brad's fiancée had been very particular about what she wanted each and every person to wear, including me, Brad's best man.

Normally, I'd have told Brad to tell his fiancée to fuck off. My closet back at my penthouse was lined with top of the line tuxedos that would beat anything worn by men from either side of their families. I didn't have to wear something else just because Brad's prissy fiancée had control issues.

But it would be the best best day of his life, or the worst day, depending on which way you looked at it, so I felt I'd swallow my pride just this once just to make them both happy. I was doing this because I knew that if Katie was happy, Brad was happy, and life would be much easier for him.

There was also another reason why I decided to entertain Katie's power play. Charles Whitmore was supposed to be delivering a presentation in the boardroom today. To keep from losing my cool, I'd taken the day off and decided to come check out how my investment in Brad's wedding was coming along. I wouldn't be able to tolerate looking into the faces of the men who wanted to replace me and listen to Charles without wanting to smash their faces in.

As I continued to observe members of Brad and Katie's family filing through the hall, I noticed a girl with long, dirty-blonde hair that made my mouth go dry. With a clipboard clutched in her hands while she motioned someone over to the dressing room, she was wearing a tight red dress that emphasized her curvy frame and white heels. She had a pretty face, proportionate breasts and a nice ass.

31

After a moment, I couldn't help it and I found myself inching across the room to get closer. She was just finishing pointing someone over to a group of workers when I walked up.

"Busy directing the troops?" I asked.

She looked up at me as I towered over her, and her lips parted in surprise and then a blush brought color to her cheeks. I hid my grin.

She peered at her clipboard she was holding, probably to conceal her embarrassment, and then looked back at me. "Are you one of the wedding guests?" she asked. I liked her voice, soft but firm at the same time, really pleasant to the ears. Her eyes, which were a bright green color, captivated me with their vivaciousness.

"Yeah, the best man," I replied.

Surprise etched across her face. "Oh, oh," she said breathlessly. "April is going to want to do your measurements." She scribbled something down on her clipboard and then looked back at me. "What is your name?"

"Tyler Locklin."

A small gasp escaped her lips and I wondered what was wrong.

"Tyler Locklin?" she asked as if unsure of what she'd just heard.

"Yeah. Is that some sort of a crime?" I joked.

"No, not at all," she said quickly. "I just didn't expect for you to be here."

And I wouldn't be if it weren't for Brad's neurotic fiancée, I thought to myself.

"Someone's got to make sure everything is going to

plan," I said. I really liked the girl's lips. They were sassy and sensual, and I knew I had to have her.

At that moment, April chose to walk over. "I can help you now, Mr. Locklin. If you would just come right this way—"

"Actually," I interrupted. I looked over the blonde girl and quickly caught her name tag. *Victoria*. "Victoria here was going to help me with my measurements."

I even like her name.

A shocked expression marred Victoria's pretty face. "I was?"

I nodded. "That's what we were just talking about, remember?"

Victoria opened her mouth to protest further, but I gave her a look that made her pause.

"That was supposed to be my job," said April. She looked disappointed as she eyed me.

"I know, but Victoria and I go way back. I think I'll be most comfortable taking my pants off in front of her." It was hard not to laugh as Victoria's eyes grew as wide as saucers.

"Wow, I didn't know you knew Mr. Locklin, Victoria." April chewed on her bottom lip, debating with herself. "Fine," she said finally. "If that's what you prefer, Mr. Locklin, I'm sure Victoria will be more than happy to accommodate."

"It is . . . and she will," I replied with confidence. I turned to Victoria and offered her my arm, unable to keep myself from smirking. "If you'd just lead the way, Miss Victoria."

Victoria was flustered, her cheeks a dark shade of red as she glanced back and forth between April and me. After a moment, she finally took my arm and began to lead me toward the dressing rooms.

April tried to mutter under her breath to Victoria as we walked off, but I still managed to catch what she said. "You'd better not screw this up, Vicky."

"Why did you lie to her?" Victoria demanded as soon as we were out of earshot. She let go of my arm and put distance between us. I wasn't worried. She'd be begging for it before I was done with her.

"Because you look like the girl for the job."

She scowled at me, her cheeks turning crimson. "What the hell is that supposed to mean?"

"Just that it looks like you can handle big things."

Victoria appeared speechless and it was hard not to laugh.

"My size," I clarified. "I'm a pretty tall guy."

I wondered if her face would remain permanently red as she simply said, "Oh."

We made it to a vacant dressing room and stepped inside. Victoria closed the door behind us. There were a bench, a mirror and a hanger rack in the room. She walked over and sat her clipboard down on the bench and then turned to face me with measuring tape.

"Do you do this often?" I asked before we got down to business. I was intrigued by Victoria and wanted to know more about her.

Victoria shook her head. "Only when I'm called to, which is rarely. This wedding demanded a lot of fittings, so Christine sent a small army to help out." She shook her head. "But I didn't expect that I'd end up fitting you."

"Why are you so surprised?"

"Well, for one, I hear that you're some big shot."

I nodded. I'm not very humble, so I wasn't going to act like I was. "I'm the co-founder, along with my father."

Victoria fingered the measuring tape. "That's amazing. You look young. How old are—"

"Twenty-five," I replied.

She shook her head. "I'm just twenty-two. I couldn't fathom accomplishing what you have at that age."

"I did have a lot of help from my father," I admitted. "From a young age, he's groomed me in business and economics. But I've grown into my own man now."

"I see." After a moment of awkward silence, Victoria cleared her throat and said, "I'm going to need you to take your shirt off."

I was happy to oblige. I slowly unbuttoned my dress shirt, staring at Victoria all the while. I slipped it off my shoulders and tossed it on the bench, my washboard abs proudly on display.

Victoria stared at the muscles etched across my stomach for a moment, and I didn't miss the flash of admiration in her eyes before she stepped forward with the measuring tape. I tried not to smile as I noted her trembling hands.

"Can you raise your arms above your head?" she asked. Even her voice had a slight tremor in it.

I did as she asked and she moved in close, wrapping the tape around my torso. I peered down as she worked, noting the fullness of her hair. Up close, I could smell the fragrance she had on, a pleasant peach-like scent that reminded me of a fresh summer day.

"You have a nice, slim waist," she said quietly with admiration as she worked. I liked when her hands brushed across my skin. They felt soft and pleasant. "But broad shoulders. Are you a swimmer?"

"I work out a lot and jog," I replied. "At least five times a week."

"I can see that," she said after she'd moved up and down my torso three times. She moved back over to the bench and picked up her clipboard, scribbling something down. Then she turned back around to face me, biting her lower lip.

"What?" I ask when she just stood there looking nervous.

"Uh, I could get a more accurate measurement if you take off your pants," she finally blurted out. "But it's totally up to you . . . and leave your underwear on," she amended quickly when I begin to tug at my dress pants.

I grinned at her and dropped my trousers to the floor. Now I was in nothing but my boxers with a cute girl staring at my junk.

"T-T-This will only take a moment," she stammered, her eyes flitting away from my crotch area. I had to grin. I was so enjoying this.

She approached me slowly and then bent over slightly to wrap the measuring tape around my inner thigh. Her hands were inches away from my junk and it was an effort not to pop wood right in her face.

"Even your thighs are muscular," she muttered in awe.

"Wouldn't it be better if you got on your knees?" I asked her when she appeared to be having trouble getting her measurement.

She paused as if shocked by my suggestion. "I'm good," she replied shortly.

"Then why are your hands shaking?"

"I'm just a little nervous, that's all."

I shifted on my feet, my cock and balls coming dangerously close to touching her hand. "I know what will help you relax."

She peered up at me. "What?"

"Has anyone ever told you that you have nice, dick-sucking lips?" I asked. I had no idea where the hell that came from. Of course I was thinking it, but I didn't exactly mean to blurt it out.

Victoria straightened all the way. "Excuse me?" Her voice, which had been soft, was now hard and filled with hostility.

I stood there for a moment, not sure if I should try to lie my way out of my flub. Fuck it. Might as well roll with it.

"You have nice lips," I compliment. "They'd look good wrapped around my dick."

"Fuck you!"

The smack of flesh was loud, but I barely felt it as my head snapped slightly to the side.

Victoria didn't wait around for my response. Scrambling quickly, she gathered her stuff and then ran out of the dressing room.

Victoria

He's a pig. A freaking handsome pig, but a pig nonetheless. What's worse is that I couldn't stop thinking about him or his amazing body. I could still see his chiseled frame in front of my eyes.

And I didn't want to think about how good looking he was, with his strong jawline that looked sharp enough to cut glass and his incredible, deep-set blue eyes that made me want to swim in them. And the way his lips curled up into that playful grin that said he was a mischievous bastard? *Shit.*

And I can't forget his scent. My God, what it did to me. When I was up close on him, all I could smell was pure masculinity. The scent had been like a powerful aphrodisiac. It made me dizzy with lust.

What made me even more mad at myself is that I'd wanted, more than anything, to see what lay underneath his boxers. If the bulge that he sported had been any indication, then Mr. Tyler Locklin was carrying around a monster.

I was pissed at myself for being attracted to him. I'd never had a guy talk so boldly like that to me before, and by default, I shouldn't be having sinful thoughts about him. But being enclosed with him inside that small dressing room made me weak in the knees.

Inside, he'd radiated a cool confidence and power that overwhelmed my senses. And when I saw him drop his dress pants . . .

I angrily pushed the lustful thoughts away and tried to get as far away from the dressing room as possible.

It was only after I was in the middle of the hall that I

realized what I'd done. I slapped Tyler Locklin. It wouldn't be so bad—he'd definitely been asking for it—if he wasn't some powerful executive that happened to be paying my boss an obscene amount of money to outfit an entire wedding!

There's no way I'm going back to apologize, I told myself. *He totally deserved it.*

I suddenly jumped at April's voice. "Did you get Mr. Locklin's measurements?"

I turned around and saw April holding a pile of things in her arms. "For the most part," I said.

April gawked at me. "What the hell do you mean?"

"Look, I couldn't help it. The guy is a total asshole!"

April glanced at the dressing room Tyler and I were in. "What are you talking about? It seemed like you two were friends?"

I scowled. "I don't know him. It's just some crap he made up. He's just some arrogant, rich prick." I shook my head angrily. "I can totally see why Christine said he was going to lose his job."

"Hey Ladies," Tyler broke in. He'd snuck up on us. I would never admit it, but I loved the deep, rich timbre of his voice. It was so sexy . . .

"How's everything going?" His eyes sparkled with mischief as he looked at me as if the dressing room fiasco had never happened. He didn't appear to be mad that I'd slapped him, which was a relief, because I feared that he'd go back and tell Christine.

"It's going well. We almost have everyone's measurements and are just waiting for the last few stragglers to show up." April looked at me uncertainly, then back at Tyler, unsure what to think. "Everything went well with your measuring, I hope?"

Tyler nodded, his eyes still on me. I had to look away. His gaze was so hot that it made me feel like I'd catch fire. "Victoria is very good with her hands."

I was speechless at Tyler's audacity.

April beamed. "That's wonderful!"

"Yep. We had so much fun catching up on our past that she's meeting me at Roxy's at eight tomorrow night."

This time I nearly choked on my surprise, and Tyler only smiled wider at my reaction.

"Wow." April tossed me an envious gaze, seemingly not noticing that my mouth was open so wide that an elephant could jump through it. Then she gestured at a group of workers nearby. "Can I show you what Christine has planned before we leave?"

"Certainly." Tyler turned to me and tossed me a playful wink. "Catch you later, Victoria." He walked off with April, leaving me standing there in disbelief.

Did he really think I was going to show up at Roxy's tomorrow?

"Who the hell was that!" I heard Gabe exclaim behind me.

I swirled around to see him staring in Tyler's direction.

"That," I said, "Is Tyler Locklin. A rich, misogynistic pig." Gabe stared at me. "Why do you say that?"

I proceeded to tell Gabe what happened in the dressing room, making sure to leave out my extreme attraction to him.

"That's all he said?" Gabe asked. "And you're pissed off about that? Girl, you should've told him to whip it out!"

I rolled my eyes. I should've known better than to expect sympathy from Gabe. "Not a chance."

Gabe turned his eyes back on Tyler. "I wish he'd say that to me. Damn, he's hot AND rich; doesn't get any better."

"Gabe!" I protested.

"What? It's the truth!"

"He asked me out," I said a second later.

Gabe turned on me, wide-eyed. "He did?"

I nodded. "But I don't think I'm going to go. Not after how he treated me."

Gabe scowled at me. "Are you crazy? You'd better go. He's a wealthy man. Think about it for a second."

It will never be serious anyway, I thought to myself. *Because he's obviously a womanizing pig.*

I decided that I was wasting my time. Gabe would never see from my point of view. "I've got to finish up my tasks before we pack up," I said.

I walked off before he could offer a protest, and tried to push images of Tyler's chiseled torso and large bulge from my mind.

* * *

Tyler

I stepped into my dad's office and gently shut the door behind me. "You rang?"

Dressed in one of his tailor made business suits, my dad

was standing before his office window with a glass in his hand and the other stuffed in his pocket. He turned around, and I didn't miss the spark of rage that flashed in his eyes.

This would be a good meeting.

"Where were you today?" He asked quietly. I could tell by the tone of his voice that he was super fucking pissed. Exactly what I wanted.

I eased into the office, stopping near his desk. "I was at the Promade, getting fitted."

Dad frowned. "Getting fitted? What the hell for?"

"You know Brad? Well, he's getting married to the love of his life, except he couldn't afford to pay for the wedding his fiancée wanted. So I offered to fund all of it, including tailor made suits and dresses made by Christine Finnerman."

My father's lips curled up in contempt. "You took off an important day for something that could be done at any time?"

"Not any time. I'd scheduled fittings for two days. It was either today or tomorrow. I chose today." I shrugged my shoulders.

The veins stood out on his neck. He was boiling. "We had a meeting today. Charles Whitmore spoke."

I nodded. "I'm aware of that. In fact, it was the reason I took off. I can't tolerate two seconds of that blowhard."

My father gripped his glass so hard I thought it might break. "His presentation involved some important revelations about our company!"

"And your point is?"

"That you're being a difficult son of a bitch." My dad stopped himself and closed his eyes. He sucked in a deep breath and then slowly let it out. When he reopened his eyes, they were more focused. "Tyler, there's going to be a vote," he said quietly.

"On?" I asked, though I knew the answer.

"Your removal."

I knew the words were coming, but it hit me like a punch in the gut. It was my turn to get pissed. "Do you really want to do this, Dad?" I asked. "Because this can get really messy."

He stared at me unblinking, unperturbed by my threat. "I'm sorry, son . . . but you leave me no other choice. Your cavalier attitude about the company and your contempt for the rules have shown that you're unfit."

I snorted with disgust. "And Charles Whitmore is?" He opened his mouth to reply, but I interrupted. "You know what? Don't even bother. If you try to remove me, I'll make sure to make your life a living hell."

My words didn't produce a visible reaction, but I knew he was simmering with anger.

"See you in the boardroom," I said.

Then I turned and walked out.

Chapter 6
Victoria

It was an hour until eight. I was at home in my small apartment, which cost an overpriced arm and a leg. I was standing in front of my bedroom mirror, arguing with myself. I couldn't decide if I was going to go to meet Tyler or not. I'd had a particularly stressful day at work with Christine sending me all over the building for menial tasks.

I'd pissed her off because I spilled her morning coffee all over her cashmere sweater. I thought for sure I was fired in that moment, and I'm sure she was tempted, but she probably figured it would be more fun to continue torturing and humiliating me.

With the stress of the day still weighing on my shoulders, I felt like I needed a release.

But that wasn't the real reason why I was so conflicted. Images of Tyler's rippling abs and muscular body continued to torment me, filling me with a burning lust that was both startling and exciting.

During my high school and college years, I'd had a couple of boyfriends, but nothing that ever amounted to anything. Most of the relationships had ended in heartache.

And none of my boyfriends had the ridiculous confidence—and overpowering arrogance—that Tyler did. Arrogance that should have repelled me from him, but instead drew me to him like a moth to a flame.

He's rich, powerful and handsome, I told myself. *And he wants me to go on a date with him. What harm can come from it? It's not like he's asking me to marry him, and it's likely he's just looking to have a little fun. After all the stress I've been going through working for Christine, shouldn't I have a little playtime for myself?*

Images of his chiseled features, playful grin and incredibly sexy blue eyes flashed before me.

"Screw it," I said finally, making my decision. I pulled open the closet and began searching for something sexy to wear. "I'm going."

Tyler

When Victoria came strutting into Roxy's in a tight black dress and heels, I felt a grin form on my face. I knew she couldn't resist.

Roxy's was a happening little bar in the middle of downtown. Bumping music, undulating bodies, swirling, colored lights and hazy smoke made the atmosphere intoxicating.

I was sitting in the V.I.P section that overlooked most of the place with the rest of the high-rollers, dressed in expensive silk slacks and a white shirt that was unbuttoned at the top.

I watched as Victoria glided through the crowd of twisting bodies, obviously searching for me. I walked over to the edge of the section and waved. After a moment, she noticed me and began to make her way over.

"I'm glad you could make it," I yelled over the music when she reached me. I gave her a disarming smile, and

45

surprisingly, she smiled back. Still, her eyes seemed to say, *I don't trust you as far as I can throw you.*

It was hard not to ogle her body. Her tits and that ass, Mmm. I wanted to take her in the back and fuck the stubbornness out of her.

"I almost didn't come," she shouted. I noticed her makeup and found that I liked it. Smokey eye shadow decorated her lids, a faint blush on her cheeks and shiny lip gloss.

If only they were wrapped around my dick.

The image of her bent over me in the dressing room flashed before my eyes. I pushed the image away from my mind and gestured at our table.

"Come have a seat."

I walked her over to our booth and pulled out a chair. She mouthed thank you to me and sat down. I took my seat and then signaled for service.

"What will you two have?" the girl asked loudly when she stepped over. With long blonde hair and holding a serving tray in her right hand, she was dressed in a tight black skirt and a white blouse open at the front that displayed her big, and obviously fake, tits. I didn't bother looking at the bait, only having eyes for Victoria. Besides, a bimbo like her came a dime a dozen and I could fuck her anytime if I wanted.

"Johnnie Walker Blue," I said.

"Apple Martini."

"So what made you decide to come?" I asked, making sure to keep my voice loud enough so she could hear me. "I thought I'd really pissed you off back at the Promade."

Victoria brushed a stray strand of hair out of her eyes. "I

thought I'd come to give you a chance to apologize."

I hid a grin. "Well, you won't get one. Because I meant what I said."

She scowled at me and shook her head. "I should have known."

"What? I gave you a compliment."

"It was crude," she objected. "And distasteful."

The girl walked over and set down our drinks. She made sure to bend low, putting her tits in my face. I ignored them and tossed her a tip.

Her eyes widened with surprise. "Thanks, handsome."

Victoria rolled her eyes as the waitress blew a seductive kiss my way and strutted away. The bass from the music moved our glasses across the table. In unison, we grabbed our drinks to keep them from toppling over.

"Did you really have to tip her so much?" She was irritated, though she tried to hide it. I found it cute.

"I always tip big wherever I go," I told her. "It's a matter of style."

"She looked like she wanted to sleep with you after."

I nodded. "That's because she did."

Victoria snorted and rolled her eyes. "You're impossible."

I couldn't hold back my grin. "I'm addictive, that's what I am. I'm like a chocolate craving. You're not getting rid of me until you've had your fill."

She rolled her eyes again. "Don't flatter yourself."

I settled back in my chair and took a sip of my drink, keeping my eyes focused on Victoria. "So, tell me, what brings you to the big city to work for the one and only Christine

Finnerman?"

Victoria toyed with her drink. "I've always dreamed of working in fashion since I was a little girl. When I was younger, I would make outfits and wear them, pretending I was on the runway. My mom doesn't much approve. She thinks I'm making a huge mistake for whatever reason."

"That sucks," I remarked. I was surprised she was being open with me about it, but I liked it.

Victoria nodded. "Yeah. But then she goes on to divorce my father to marry some rich douchebag." She made an angry face. "I'm still pissed off at her about that."

"Who did she marry?"

Victoria shrugged and took a sip of her drink. I tried not to look at her lips wrapped around her straw. "Beats me. I no longer talk to her. We had a huge falling out."

"Sounds like me."

Victoria was intrigued. "How's that?"

For a moment, I debated on whether to tell her the truth. I'm usually not one to open up so easily.

Screw it, I said to myself.

"My father is a man of voracious appetite. As in, he's never been satisfied being with one woman. He claims he's done with all of that now, but we'll see. Anyway, to make a long story short, my mom found out about one of his flings, and she decided to divorce him. Naturally, since we were close, my mother thought I would pressure my dad to hand over his share of the business to her when they split. Instead, I helped my dad buy my mom's cooperation. This infuriated my mother and we grew apart, but I couldn't help it. I'd put too much of myself in the business, and I couldn't see it growing without the both of us. Now . . . I'm having second thoughts about that."

Victoria raised an eyebrow and I proceeded to tell her all about the growing rift between my father and me.

"And the funny thing is," I said when I was finished telling her my story, "he wants me to get my act together when he's been the worst offender of all." I shook my head. "I feel sorry for the woman he married . . . but then again, she probably didn't marry him for his personality."

Victoria stared at me. "What's so bad about it, though? Settling down. I mean, how can it be fun to sleep around all the time?"

Anger twisted my stomach. "I've had a bad relationship in the past that taught me that love is just a made-up notion that's more trouble than it's worth."

Damn it. I shouldn't be telling her this.

"I see."

We both stopped speaking and the bass of the music filled in the silence.

"I just don't see why you would continue doing what you do if you know it effects your company," she said a moment later.

I leaned across the table and looked her straight in the eye. "Because no one tells me what to do."

Victoria stared at me for a long time before saying, "I shouldn't have come."

"Then why did you?"

"I'm not sure. But I wish I hadn't told you anything. You probably have a line of skanks lined up after this."

49

I shook my head and then downed my drink in one gulp. I let out a satisfied sigh as my throat burned and stood up. I offered my hand to Victoria. "Come, I want to show you something."

She looked at me like I was crazy. "I'm not going anywhere with you."

"Yeah you are, or you wouldn't have come. Now get up."

A tremble went through her at the authority in my voice and I knew she liked it. Finally, she gave up the act and took my hand, but before she stood up, she asked, "Where are we going?"

I grinned at her and pulled her to her feet. "Some place where you can finish measuring me."

Chapter 7
Victoria

"It's breathtaking!" I exclaimed as I stepped inside.

I was in Tyler's ritzy loft overlooking the city, and I was immediately captivated by what was before me. The right side of the apartment had a wall made out of glass that looked out into the shimmering skyline. You could see for what seemed like forever. The view took my breath away.

I turned about, taking in the rest of the apartment.

It had a spacious floor plan that gave a warm, inviting feeling. The floor was made of polished wood that looked like it'd been freshly mopped. He probably had maids that kept the place spotless. The sofa and lounge seats were all cream-colored and looked lush and comfortable. Near the window, there was a white grand piano.

This, I said to myself as I took everything in, *is what I want. This is how I want to live. Except I'll never get here working for Christine.*

"Is it?" Tyler asked as he walked over to the kitchen's bar and began tinkering with some glasses. "I paid enough for it, so it had better be."

I knew better than to ask how much. I probably didn't want to know. I walked over to the window and stared out while Tyler busied himself. "I could learn to love this," I whispered, my heart soaring at the incredible view. Tyler's place made my tiny downtown apartment look like a hovel. Now I'd never view it the same again.

"Would you like something to drink?" Tyler asked me.

I half-turned, debating. I was already feeling a little tipsy from my martini and I didn't want to do something stupid.

"No thanks," I declined. "I'm good."

Tyler peered at me. "You sure?"

"Positive."

He finished making a drink and walked over to me with a glass of clear liquid, his shoes making a hard tapping sound against the floor.

I turned back to the view and shook my head. "This place really is incredible. I've set some goals for myself, but I can't imagine ever being in a place like this. I can barely afford a one-bedroom apartment on the salary Christine pays me."

Tyler reached my side and I could smell the alcohol in his glass. The smell was so strong it made my nostrils burn. I wondered what was in it.

"Why do you work for her?" He stared out the window with me while taking a sip from his glass.

I sighed. "I'm hoping that doors will open for me. There's a lot you can do with Christine Finnerman's name on your resume. If you're interested in fashion, there's no better place to start."

He turned to study me. "Do you really believe it'll pay off?

I thought for a moment. The fact is, I really didn't know. It's just what I hoped for. "I have to believe that it will."

"Sometimes believing isn't enough. Sometimes you gotta

know."

"Well, sometimes you can't know, so believing is all that you can do."

Tyler's gaze became so intense that I could feel my skin crawl. "That's not good enough for me."

I shivered underneath his gaze, but I couldn't help thinking about all the women he must bring to this place. "Is anything ever good enough for you?"

"You."

My heart skipped a beat and my mouth went dry. Tyler moved in and I hesitantly backed up against the window. The glass slipped from his hand and shattered against the floor, but I hardly noticed it.

He reached over and ran his hand down my arm, caressing my skin softly. I trembled at his touch. It felt amazing.

"What are you doing?" I managed.

Tyler paused, his hand on my wrist. "What do you think?"

"I didn't come here to let you take me to bed," I said.

"You didn't?" He had that playful grin on his face that I found so damn irresistible. "What did you think I was bringing you back here for? To bake s'mores?" He ran a finger up my arm, all the way up my shoulder and then my neck. He stopped at my neck as if he was counting my heartbeat.

"I-I-I'm not one of your whores," I stammered, my heart hammering within my chest.

"I never said you were," Tyler said, coming in close. The heat from his body was enough to send me up into flames. The next thing I knew, his burning lips were on my neck and I threw my head back against the window, letting out a giant sigh.

I shouldn't be doing this, I told myself frantically. *I don't know this man.*

But I couldn't move. Tyler had claimed me, and my body was his playground. His hands roamed down to my breasts and he squeezed them slightly before moving down to the hem of my dress.

He moved his lips to mine and slipped his tongue into my mouth. We kissed with passion as he grabbed my legs and hoisted me onto his waist, pressing my ass cheeks up against the window. It felt incredible, and any resistance I felt was washed away from the powerful lust coursing through my body.

If there was anyone who could see us in the surrounding hi-rise buildings, they had a wonderful view of my ass.

I was surprised when Tyler let me go, dropping me back to my feet, and knelt down before me. Looking up at me with that intense gaze, he raised my dress up to my abdomen, revealing my panties. He sniffed once, as if inhaling my scent, then he pulled them down, tossing them onto the wooden floor.

He placed his hands on my moist mound and I groaned. He slid a single finger inside and I gasped as he probed the inside of my canal for a moment before taking it back out. Even I could see the juices covering his finger. I was already soaking wet.

Looking up at me, he stuck his finger in his mouth and sucked on it.

"Sweet," he growled.

He took two of his fingers and spread my lips wide open like a butterfly, and began licking forcefully, sending me to cloud nine. While he licked, he stuck a finger back inside, sliding it in and out. Slowly, he added another.

The sensation was incredible. I could hardly take it as he thrust in and out, now with three fingers. Wet, *plop* sounds filled the loft as he wiggled his fingers inside of me, scattering my juices all over my thighs. A force was building inside my stomach. I reached down and held onto his shoulders, weak in the knees, almost collapsing against the window.

He looked at me with a feral scowl. I felt like he was a wild animal, claiming me as his property as he pumped deep inside of me.

Finally, I could take no more. A raw scream escaped my throat. It was so loud that I thought his neighbors could hear me. Too bad. My limbs rippled from the powerful sensation coursing through my body.

Slowly, Tyler pulled his fingers out. They were covered by my juices and he licked at his fingers like an animal.

He rose to his feet and grabbed onto me. I was still weak from my mind-blowing orgasm, but he didn't care. He walked me over to the couch and bent me over. I could hear the sound of him unzipping his pants, and then I thought I heard the sound of him ripping open a package. I'm sure he was well-stocked.

He entered me and I gasped as he felt incredibly large. My juices quickly lubricated him, and he began to pound into me as I dug my fingernails into the couch, barely able to take him.

While he hammered into me, he pulled my dress all the way above my breasts and snatched off my bra, grabbing onto my nipples and twisting them. I gasped in pain, and all I could hear was the sound of smacking flesh filling the room as his chiseled thighs smacked into my ass.

A fire was building in my stomach again. I was on the brink of an incredible orgasm, more crazy than the last. Before I could come, Tyler pulled out. I tried to turn around, but he held me against the couch.

"Beg for it," he commanded me.

I needed his magnificent tool, which I still hadn't seen, back inside me. My body craved it. But my pride was getting in the way.

"No," I said angrily.

He pulled me up against his body and placed his hand around my throat from behind me. I could feel his hard cock throbbing against my back. The pulses were strong and powerful.

"Beg for it," he repeated, his breath hot on my neck. He took his other hand and grabbed my breast, squeezing it firmly.

I leaned my head back into him and moaned. His touch felt incredible.

"Do it," he insisted. When I didn't immediately comply, he pushed me forward over the couch and took his dick and smacked my ass with it. Then he teased his head around my entry, rubbing me with the tip.

"Oh God. Give it to me please!" I cried.

"Louder."

"Fuck me!" I yelled.

My eyes went wide and I gasped when he thrust himself balls deep inside of me. This time, he pounded me with incredible force while holding onto my waist. I knew that I was going to be sore, but I didn't care. My body was on fire and it felt so fucking good.

His grip on my waist tightened, so hard that it was painful. Inside, I could feel his cock grow even harder. I knew he was going to come soon, and so was I.

His breathing became labored and heavy, his thrusts slower and deliberate. Before he could climax, I came first, screaming like a psycho, digging my fingernails into the couch.

Tyler was next. One powerful thrust, and he collapsed against my back with a grunt, his sweat melding with mine, his cock contracting powerfully inside of me. He held me there for a few moments in a seductive silence.

I couldn't believe what I'd done. I was only supposed to be going to Roxy's to have a little fun, not end up back at his place becoming one of his new conquests.

You made a big mistake, Vicky, I told myself.

But didn't I deserve it? The sex had been incredible. Mind-blowing. *Addicting.*

Tyler apparently wasn't done with me just yet. He pulled out of me and straightened. I stood up, my insides feeling sore, and I turned around. Tyler still had his shirt on, though unbuttoned, showing off his incredible abs that were slick with his sweat, and his pants pooled at the bottom of his legs. His cock, semi-flaccid, was as big as I thought it would be, with a huge, luscious head. The condom he was wearing hung half off his shaft, almost filled to the brim with fluid.

He stepped out of his pants, took me by the hand, and led me up the winding stairs. The top of the stairs let out into a large room that was black and grey. A king-size bed stood before us, welcoming and inviting.

This is my time to say that I need to go, I said to myself, *and forget that this ever happened.*

"Maybe I should go," I said.

Tyler pushed me toward the bed. "I can't allow that." Slowly, he peeled off the condom and then walked over to the wastebasket and tossed it inside.

"I can run out of here if I want to," I threatened.

He walked back over in front of me and grinned. "Try it."

I didn't move. I was such a wimp.

"On your knees," he commanded.

I hesitated. Who did he think he was? And how the hell could he possibly be recovered in five minutes?

"Now!" he roared.

Despite his tone, I giggled until I was laughing so hard my sides hurt. He stalked forward and grabbed me. "You think it's funny?" he growled at me. I was ashamed to admit it, but I was turned on to the max. "Get on your fucking knees."

"Make me," I said fearlessly to his face.

He pushed me down so fast I had no time to react. On my knees, I was level with his dick. Up close, oh my, it seemed even bigger than before, and my mouth was watering for it. I stared at it longingly, even noting his chiseled thighs surrounding it. I ran my hand up his thigh, marveling at the power in them.

I had to admit, Tyler was the epitome of male masculinity. Powerful and magnificent.

"Now show me what you can do with those lips."

Before I knew it, he was inside of my mouth and I was

close to gagging. Above me, he let out a groan. I pulled back on his shaft to gain respite, sucking gently on his huge head. It didn't take long before he was back rock hard again.

Eager for more, Tyler placed a hand behind my head and guided me along his shaft. It was hard for me to take all of him, but I did the best I could. I used my right hand to fondle his balls. They felt huge and full—surprising after the load he'd just emptied.

His head felt like it hit the back of my throat and I almost gagged. I pulled away and gasped for breath. This whole time I'm thinking, *I can't believe I'm doing this*.

Tyler only let me get a couple of breaths in before he was back inside of my mouth, thrusting and pumping. His powerful thigh muscles flexed in front of my face as he forcefully pushed inside.

Before long, he was bucking inside of my mouth, testing my gag reflex to the limits, using my mouth like his personal fuck box. I struggled to breathe and to not gag as he held me in place to keep me from gaining a respite.

He let out a feral groan and I felt him growing harder and firmer in my mouth. I knew he was about to come. I couldn't allow him to empty himself down my throat. I wasn't going to let him win.

I could feel his cock pulsating as it rubbed along my tongue, ready to burst. At the last possible second, I jerked away and Tyler gasped.

He was forced to finish himself off and he blew his load all over the floor. Rising to my feet, I watched in fascination as he threw his head back, his muscles rippling, his washboard stomach contracting in and out while he stroked every last drop out of his huge balls.

When he was done, he let out a sigh and straightened before looking at me. I tried not to glance at the mess on the floor, and I wondered who'd clean it up.

"You pulled away," he said in an accusatory tone. "You weren't supposed to."

"Yeah," I replied. "I wasn't going to let you come in my mouth. What do you think I am?"

He walked over to me and grabbed me by the hair. "You have a tart little mouth on you, you know that?"

* * *

I came awake with a gasp. I was still in Tyler's bed, naked as the day I was born. I ran my hand through the soft, rumpled covers, searching. Tyler was gone. I didn't know if he was in the bathroom or what. I just knew my body felt sore all over.

"I see he's brought another one home," said a deep voice.

Startled, I looked up.

Dressed in fancy clothing, there was an older, grey-haired man standing at the edge of the stairs, staring at me.

I stared back at him, mouth wide, when I suddenly realized that I was naked. I quickly snatched the covers and held them to my breasts.

"Who are you?" I demanded, frightened.

"Jonathan, Mr. Locklin's butler." Jonathan nodded his head back down the stairs. "I saw you two when you came in."

My throat was suddenly dry. "Did you see us . . ." my words trailed off.

"Having sex?" Jonathan let out a chuckle. "Heavens, no. I'd never do that."

I looked around, wondering why the hell Tyler's butler was in his room staring at me. I decided that it didn't matter. It was probably time for me to get my shit and leave, but the problem was, my car was still at Roxy's. Tyler drove us here.

"You're wondering why I'm here," he says at the confusion on my face.

Slowly, I nodded, watching him closely.

"I'm here to offer you a ride back home or to your car . . . whichever you may prefer." He chuckled. "Tyler refers to the custom as *the Drop Off.*"

Anger swirled within me and I clutched the covers with fury. Tyler had sex with me and now was disposing of me like everyone else. I should've known better.

I knew I shouldn't have come here! I raged at myself.

No matter how pissed I got at myself and Tyler, it was no less than I deserved. I mean, who goes on a date with someone who insults them on the very first day they meet, and then goes and has sex with them after?

A desperate one.

Or a really deprived girl, I thought to myself.

Ever since working for Christine, I never got to go out and enjoy anything for myself, nor had I had any real dates in ages. I suppose a momentary lapse of judgment could be excused if I hadn't lain down with the womanizer from hell.

But the sex had been good—mind-blowingly good—and I had enjoyed every moment of it.

It was just sex, I told myself. *Nothing more, nothing less. I need to walk out of here and forget about it and forget about him.*

"You're angry," Jonathan noted, pulling me out of my reverie. "Don't be."

I knew I shouldn't reveal my feelings to a stranger, but I couldn't help myself. "I just can't believe how he can just . . ."

"Use you and then just leave?" Jonathan offered.

I nodded my head.

He walked over and sat down on the edge of the bed. Normally I'd be jumping away, but he seemed sincere. "Honey, he does it to every girl that walks through that door." Jonathan pauses as if debating on whether he should continue speaking. "But walking through that door and never coming back is the best thing that will ever happen to you."

His words chilled me. "Why do you say that?"

He looked at me and I could see sadness in his eyes. "You look like a nice girl, nicer than the ones that usually come through here, and I'm sure you have a bright future ahead of you."

"You didn't answer my question," I say firmly.

Jonathan stared at me and then let out a sigh. "Mr. Locklin has a past."

My heart skipped a beat. "What kind of past?"

Jonathan took a long time to reply. "I don't know if I should be saying this, but Tyler's a scarred young man. Nothing a lot of men don't go through at some point in their lives, but he took it hard, and because of this, he never stays with any woman for long. Most of them only get one night, two or three at most, but never much longer than that."

Knowing that Tyler is a womanizer, I should have

understood this. But then why am I getting so mad about it? It didn't help matters that his butler was acting so mysteriously about him.

When I got right down to it, I didn't really know who Tyler Locklin was and had no business in his place.

"I think I've heard enough," I said finally, looking around for my dress. "I'm ready to go now."

Chapter 8
Tyler

I couldn't stop thinking about her. It wasn't like me at all, my thoughts being consumed by a woman after a night with one. I don't know what it was about Victoria, but she put a spell on me and it frustrated the hell out of me.

For the longest time, I'd been able to sleep with girls and leave them without a second thought. Now, it was hard to get through the day without thinking about her—her smile, her curvy figure, and most of all, her headstrong personality. Not only that, but hearing her story about her being estranged from both parents and struggling to make ends' meet while working for a bitchy egomaniac made me feel for her. She made me want to be a better person, a better man. To provide for her.

It frightened the shit out of me, because for the first time in my life, I felt like I was losing control.

"The board is preparing," Jeff told me.

We were sitting in the boardroom after a long day of work. My peers acted no differently with me than normal, laughing and joking and carrying on, giving no indication that they were about to vote on my removal.

But they were fools, all of them.

I'd make sure I knew everyone who was planning to vote against me. When I came out of this mess triumphant and with a smile on my face, every last one of them would pay dearly.

"They are?" I asked nonchalantly. "How convenient."

Jeff stared at me. "Aren't you a little bit worried?"

"No," I replied as I kicked my feet up onto the marble table to infuriate Jeff. "Why should I be?"

"Because Charles Whitmore is about to have your job."

He was obviously trying to piss me off by mentioning Charles, but it didn't work. After long, hard thinking, I'd come up with a plan that would make everyone happy and resolve my dilemma.

I'd made a decision.

"That's not going to happen," I said with all confidence.

Jeff raised an eyebrow. "Why not?"

It was hard for me to say my next words, but I managed it. "Because I'm ready . . . to behave.

Victoria

For the past several weeks, Tyler had taken me on a whirlwind of a romance. From upscale night clubs to expensive restaurants, Tyler took me everywhere. We were inseparable.

I had no idea why I'd accepted his offer to start dating, especially considering the warning given to me by practically everyone, but I guess I couldn't help himself.

All it had taken was a bouquet of roses, a bottle of expensive wine and Tyler's playful grin to convince me to go against what my brain was telling me.

In a way, I suppose I felt special. After all, it was rumored that Tyler didn't give a girl more than a day or two of his time, and here he was giving me weeks.

Despite the warning signs going off in the back of my mind, I was thrilled beyond belief. Here was this incredibly handsome and rich guy who could literally have any woman he wanted—and he wanted me.

And the wild, crazy sex that involved a bit of domination? I lived for it. Rough and exciting, each time was like a dangerous adventure where I never knew where I'd wind up.

I was so caught up in my new arrangement that Christine's mistreatment of me at work ceased to bother me. The only thing that mattered in my world was Tyler.

* * *

I was working with April and Gabe in the factory room, helping with the finishing touches on the wedding gown for Tyler's best friend's wedding, when a young man came walking in.

Tall, blonde and handsome, he was dressed in a business suit, and it looked as if he was looking for something, or someone.

April and Gabe were busy talking to a group of workers while they complained about a problem with a gown, and I was the only one who seemed to notice the guy, so I walked over.

"May I help you?" I asked politely.

The man looked at me for a moment and then smiled. I noticed that he had straight, white teeth. "I'm looking for Victoria Young."

What the hell could he want with me? I wondered.

"You're speaking to her."

He was surprised. "Oh." He held out his hand. "I'm

Charles Whitmore, an executive from Armex."

For some reason, his name sounded familiar, but I couldn't place it. But I did recognize the name of Tyler's company.

After a moment, I took his hand and gently shook it. He firmly had my attention now. I wondered what this was going to be about. "Nice to meet you," I said. "So what brings you here?"

And why the hell are you looking for me?

Charles shifted on his feet and then glanced over at April and Gabe. "Can we talk?"

"I'm kinda busy," I said. "If you can just tell me what this is about."

Charles gave me a look that brought me up short. "It's about Tyler."

* * *

"You're making a big mistake," Charles said to me.

We were sitting in a high-class coffee shop down the street from the corporate fashion building. He ordered me a latte that was topped by a mound of whip cream.

I played with it a little. "How's that?"

"Tyler . . . he's no good." He gestured at me. "This relationship he has going with you? It won't last."

I scowled. "I fail to see how our relationship is any of your business." Honestly, I didn't know why I agreed to talk with this Charles guy.

Jonathan's words came back to me in that moment, filling me with anxiety.

Walking through that door and never coming back is the best thing that will ever happen to you

Charles pressed his fingertips together and gave me a direct gaze. "It does when it affects my position at my company."

"What are you talking about?"

"Before you came around, Tyler was on the verge of losing his position due to his . . . uncouth behavior. He'd slept with so many women that I'm sure he lost count. His dalliances were costing us, and when confronted about it, he refused to stop—which is why we were going to vote to remove him. Then you show up, and suddenly he says he'll clean up his act."

I glared. "So what are you saying? He's just playing me?"

Charlie nodded. "Like a fiddle."

"I think I've heard about enough of this," I hissed. "I've let you waste enough of my time." I rose from my seat, my latte still untouched.

"A word of caution, Miss Young," Charles said, giving me pause. "Keep messing with Tyler, and you'll likely find yourself without a job." He looked me up and down critically. "And after everyone finds out you were Tyler's little whore, you'll only find work on the street corner with the looks you have."

His words were more than I could take. Without thinking, I grabbed the latte and splashed it all over his suit.

"Fuck you, asshole!" I growled.

Cutting my eyes, I turned and walked out, leaving him sputtering.

Charles

I wiped the whipped cream off with a napkin and cracked a smile. There was fire in that one. I could see why Tyler was intrigued with her.

My intuition told me this one wasn't quite the same; she seemed more high class. Maybe that's why Tyler was seeing her long-term—she represented a challenge.

Whatever the case, my mission was accomplished. I'd planted the seed in her mind, and her fears and insecurities would do the rest.

"Is everything alright, sir?" a light voice asked. I turned to see a waitress staring at me.

"I'm fine." I give her a smile and she smiled back.

"Why did that lady throw her latte on you?" she had to ask.

"Her boyfriend left her and she's having a mental breakdown."

"Oh that sucks. She didn't have to take it out on you, though."

I shook my head. "Nope, she didn't. So . . . what's your name?"

Chapter 9
Victoria

"We're going to meet my father," Tyler said to me.

We were riding in his limo, because Tyler had begun giving me rides to and from work in the lap of luxury. I was looking forward to going back to Tyler's place and relaxing. That dream was shattered, however, once I got in the car.

He informed me that his father wanted to meet me. Since Tyler had agreed to clean up his act, his father wanted to meet me.

I was fine with it, but I now had doubts. Warnings from Tyler's butler—and now, Charles Whitmore—had me on edge. I hadn't spoken to Tyler about either one of them . . . yet.

"Do we have to?" I asked. "I'm kinda tired."

Tyler shook his head. "It'll only take a minute. He just wants to meet you and find out a little about you."

I groaned.

Tyler placed a hand on my leg and I felt sparks through his fingertips. "Please, baby?" he asked me. "For me?"

I was shocked. I'd never heard him say please to anyone. And he topped it off with *baby*. I had to admit, I liked it.

"Say that again," I urged him.

"What?"

"Baby."

He leaned forward and kissed me softly on the lips.

"Please, baby."

I decided then that I'd do anything he asked. "All right," I said. "Whatever you want."

* * *

When Tyler and I walked into the Locklin mansion, my jaw dropped . . . and it wasn't because of the opulence of the place.

There, standing in the foyer with who I assumed was Tyler's father, was my mother, decked in expensive jewelry and an evening gown that probably cost a fortune, a wine glass in her hand.

"Victoria?" my mother exclaimed with some surprise.

"Mom?" I asked in disbelief.

The man at her side grinned. He was dressed in a suit that looked even more expensive than the one Tyler wore. "Who is this pretty young lady?"

My mother regained her composure. "James, this is Victoria, my daughter."

James walked forward and grabbed my hand. "You have your mother's beauty," he said to me.

I glanced at Tyler as a strange feeling washed over me. Something about this was all wrong. I knew this was too good to be true.

"Thank you," I replied, a slight blush coming to my cheeks. "You're too kind."

Tyler was the first to figure it out. "Wait a minute," he said. He looked at my mother, then back at me, his eyes going wide. "If this is your daughter, then that means I'm Victoria's . . ."

"Stepbrother," I whispered in horror.

Chapter 10
Victoria

Tyler walked back into his bedroom, a towel wrapped around his waist, his rippling abs moist from a recent shower. I laid in his bed, breathing in and out, recovering from a powerful orgasm.

"So what happens now?" I asked him. "We can't continue on like this."

Tyler looked at me, and I found it hard to keep my eyes from straying down to his waist. "What do you mean?" he asked.

"You're my stepbrother," I said. "Neither your dad nor my mother will approve of our relationship. They don't believe it's proper."

Tyler scowled. "Fuck what's proper. I've never obeyed the rules before, and I'm not about to now."

"But not when it comes to something like this."

Tyler walked over and sat on the bed next to me, and his towel slipped down several notches. "I'll make them get a divorce."

I sat up in the bed, shocked. "What?"

Tyler grabbed my hand and placed it on his chest. Beneath it, I could feel his heart beat. "If it'll make you feel better about being with me, and if it will take away the taboo aspect, I'll do it."

I stared at him, horrified. "You can't do that!"

"Why not? From what you say, your mother hasn't been very kind to you, and shit, my dad hasn't been anything but an asshole to me. So what's the big deal? They've screwed us over, and they're both standing in the way of what we want."

"I just can't do that," I said. "I'd never forgive myself."

Tyler became quiet. "Do you want to be with me or not?" he asked finally.

"Yes."

"Okay then." His lips found my neck, and I could only resist for one second before I gave in to his advance. "Either they're going to accept us, or I'm going to destroy them."

Chapter 11

Victoria - Two Weeks Later

'Either they're going to accept us, or I'm going to destroy them . . ."

I let out an explosive breath, my limbs wracked by powerful tremors, and clenched the bed sheets tightly beneath my nails. Wave after wave of pleasure hit me and I arched my back to the ceiling as Tyler's relentless mouth sucked on my overflowing mound.

"That was explosive." I sighed when it was over, relaxing back onto the bed. A droplet of sweat dropped from my forehead onto my exposed breasts, and I shivered at the goosebumps that covered my flesh.

With a mischievous twinkle in his eyes, Tyler looked up at me from in between my legs, an impish smile on his face, his lips wet from his meal. Oh, that smile. A smile that could break a million hearts. A smile that had stolen mine.

"There's more where that came from," Tyler assured me with confidence.

His deep baritone caused a stirring below, despite what he'd just done to me. But a deep ache warned me that I couldn't handle much more of what he could dish out.

"Oh no," I moaned weakly, "I don't think I can take anymore. Not yet."

Tyler's grin grew wider as he reared up from between my

legs, displaying his chiseled torso that glistened with sweat, and wiped my juices from his chin in one smooth motion.

"Seriously? I went easy on you, babe."

Despite my trepidation at a second round with Tyler, I was filled with overwhelming excitement over his lust for me. I'd never had a man want me so fully and utterly. *Never.*

It was still hard to believe that Tyler, an incredibly handsome, rich and eligible bachelor, would want plain old me. Me, a simple girl struggling to make ends meet, working for a ruthless, power-hungry fashion designer who would discard me as soon as I was no longer of any use to her.

What was even more unbelievable was the fact that he was my stepbrother. *My stepbrother.* The words sounded alien to me. The events that had led to this startling revelation were almost too much to process.

In the week since we'd been discovered by our parents, Tyler had gotten into several vicious arguments with his father over our relationship. In the meantime, I avoided my mother, who I'm sure had it out for me as well. I still couldn't figure out how my mom got a billionaire to marry her, but I suppose I shouldn't have been surprised. She was always good at swindling.

Either way, I wasn't going to listen to her views on my relationship with Tyler, just like I never let her dissuade me from fashion. The fact that he happened to be my stepbrother really didn't matter to me. I mean, it's not like we'd grown up together. Besides, I was angry with her for abandoning me in my time of need.

There was just one problem with my defiance—being with Tyler would most definitely cause disruption in his company. If he'd had trouble before, I could only imagine what he would be up against now.

Tyler had told me that he wasn't going down without a fight, assuring me that everything would work out in the end.

Still, I had my doubts. Related by marriage aside, maybe our relationship really wasn't for the best. Tyler was a known womanizer. I could be the flavor of the week. Was it really worth being involved in a scandal for someone who would discard me when they'd had their fill of me?

Better yet, was the drama worth the damage that our relationship was sure to cause to my career?

Tyler straddled me, bending forward to plant a steamy kiss on my lips. I would've protested—after all, he still had my juices all over his lips—but I couldn't deny the intensity of his advance.

"Come on," he urged after he pulled back, leaving me breathless. "I'm sporting some serious wood here."

I stared into his pleading eyes, my heart flipping within my chest. God, he was so handsome. So fucking sexy.

And a fucking heartbreaker, a little voice said in the back of my head. *Sure to break mine.*

It wasn't the first time that annoying little voice had reared its head. But it was hard to listen to the warnings of that voice when every molecule in my body screamed in need for this man. This sexy beast. My body refused to resist him.

"A word of caution, Miss Young. Keep messing with Tyler and you'll likely find yourself without a job. And after everyone finds out you were Tyler's whore, you'll only find work on the street corner with the looks you have."

For some reason, Charles Whitmore's smug face and insulting words popped in my mind right then, giving me the strength to push Tyler away.

"Good God! The time," I breathed, scrambling out from under a visibly disappointed Tyler and gathering my clothing scattered on the floor. "Christine is going to kill me. I'm going to be late."

Tyler sat up in the bed. "Just don't show up."

I paused, my bra in my hands, staring at Tyler with disbelief. "What?"

His eyes roved over the curves of my body, making me feel like a piece of meat.

"I've been thinking. How would you like to work for me?"

My jaw dropped. "Me?" I gasped incredulously a second later.

Tyler gave me that boyish grin that seemed to make me want to follow him to hell and back and enjoy every moment of it. "It would be the perfect opportunity for the both of us. You get to leave that demanding diva who treats you like shit, and I get to piss everyone off at the same time." He grinned wider, flashing his perfect, white teeth. "A win-win."

I should've flat out said no. "I-I don't know," I stuttered.

"Come on. I could use a smart-mouthed, hot babe like you to keep me in line."

"Is that what you really think of me? A smart-mouth?"

Tyler grinned. "Among other things, but yes."

He could insult me and make me love him for it. "Jerk."

"Seriously, though. I don't make offers like these lightly."

By the tone in Tyler's voice, I could tell he was dead serious. He really was offering me a job. "In fact, I've never offered anyone a job without going through the proper channels."

I paused, pondering the gravity of the situation. Though I'd love nothing more than to march into to Christine's office and tell her off, quitting my job with her would mean the end of my career in fashion. She would see to it. One didn't simply up and quit on Christine Finnerman.

"But my career . . ." I began to protest.

"I could help you with that."

I placed a hand on my hip and raised my brow skeptically. "How? What could you possibly know about fashion?"

"Not much."

"Okay then."

"But I don't need to. That's what you're for. I have the money to fund any projects you might want to work on to get your name out there."

The breath left my lungs. "You'd do that?" I asked in disbelief. "For me?"

Tyler nodded. "If you do as I ask." He scratched absently at his abs. "The way I see it, with my resources and your brains and knowledge of the industry," he shrugged, his voice gaining excitement as he continued speaking, "who knows? Maybe we can start a new company and I wouldn't need my father's approval. I could leave Armex and let it collapse in on itself."

I nearly swooned as the endless possibilities rolled through my mind. *I can't believe it,* I thought. *This seems too good to be true.* And you know what they say about that.

"We'll obviously have to work out the details," Tyler said, watching me intently while I stood there involved with my thoughts. "But I think we can make it work."

"So in the meantime, let's say I do come work for you. How much will you pay me?"

"Double whatever you're making now." Tyler paused to glance down mischievously, "and there are benefits."

My heart began pounding inside my chest. *This has to be some sort of a dream,* I thought, ready to pinch myself to see if I was truly awake. Tyler was offering me everything I could ever hope, or dream of . . . my own career and the man of my dreams.

"What about our parents?" I managed to ask through the turmoil rolling through my mind. "Won't my coming to work for you complicate matters even further?"

"Don't worry that pretty little head of yours. I'll take care of it," Tyler said with utmost confidence. He got up from the bed, rising like Poseidon from the sea, his magnificent body robbing me of breath. He walked over to me, wrapping his powerful arms around me. "Trust me on this," he breathed as he delivered a peck on my neck, causing the internal heat in my body to shoot up, his breath hot on my neck. "I've got it covered."

Walking through that door and never coming back is the best thing that will ever happen to you.

Jonathan's unbidden warning screamed at me to run out and never look back.

The next kiss nearly made me melt into his body, making me want to beg right then and there for him to take me again.

Run! Run far, far, far away, an errant thought cried.

And I almost did. I almost gathered the strength to push away and run. But another seductive nibble and a deft caress of my side melted any rational thought of defiance away, and I swooned as I allowed him to dip me backward and he covered my neck with passionate kisses.

Who do I think I'm fooling? He's a god. My God.

Tyler had me, hook, line and sinker.

"I'm in," I breathed.

Chapter 12
Victoria

After leaving Tyler's, I practically burned rubber to make it to work. One, because I couldn't wait to see the expression on Christine's face when I told her to eat shit and die, and two, I was thrumming with excitement over Tyler's proposal.

I can't believe it. That door that I've been waiting for has swung open! Not quite the way I'd planned, but I'll finally be free to live out my dreams!

I quickly found my usual parking space and rushed on my way. Jubilation swirled through me as I strutted inside Christine's swanky building, a giant smile on my face, my heels clicking against the floor.

"What's got you so chipper today?" a familiar voice behind me demanded as I reached the elevator. "Don't you realize you're late?"

I swirled around, only to see April peering at me suspiciously with a stack of dresses in her hand. She looked extra cute today with her hair swept up into a side pony tail, a pale blush to her cheeks and her eyelids covered in colorful shadow. Besides that, she looked practically stuffed inside the black pants that were a size too small for her. The sad thing was that she was already a size two. That's the kind of messed up crap girls did working in this industry and for Christine, who was notorious for making the girls around here feel terrible about their weight, myself included.

A smile spread across my face. "Who cares?"

April raised an eyebrow, staring at me like I'd lost my mind. "Excuse me? Christine is going to have your ass for breakfast."

"Fuck Christine."

April reared back. "Whoa. What the hell has gotten into you?"

Staring at April's shocked expression, it became too much. I burst out laughing hysterically.

"What is going on?" April demanded in concern when I doubled over, choking with laughter. "Are you on something?"

"I can't breathe," I choked, gasping for breath.

April repositioned the dresses she was holding in one arm and then pounded me on the back. After several rib aching moments, I was finally able to get myself under control.

"What the hell?" April persisted, peering me up and down as if the *real* me had vanished and had been replaced with some nut from the psych ward. "Do I need to call for help or something?"

"No. I'm fine."

"Well it doesn't seem like it," April muttered, unconvinced. "I've never seen you act like this before."

"That's because I've never been this happy in my entire life!"

"What do you mean? What's going on?"

"I'm quitting!"

April gaped. "What?"

I grinned. "It's my last day working for the unbearable

witch. The only thing I'll miss is you and Gabe, but I'm sure we'll still talk from time to time."

April frowned. "Vicky . . . are you sure about this? You're basically giving up your career if you walk out on Christine."

"No, I'm not."

"You're not? You must have really lost your mind then. Christine will make sure you never work in fashion again. You know as well as I do that she has a penchant for being vindictive."

"I won't need Christine's referrals. I'll be able to make my own work."

April peered at me warily. "Oh yeah? How's that? You're just starting out in this business with virtually no contacts. How in the world do you expect to get the resources to become successful?"

I smiled sweetly as the elevator door opened. "Tyler Locklin."

"What? Tyler Locklin—Vicky, what have you gotten yourself into?"

"Sorry, April. Gotta' go. I'm itching to tell the witch what I've been wanting to say for months. I'll be sure to stop by and tell you and Gabe bye before I leave."

"Vicky, wait! You're making a very big mistake!"

The elevator doors slid closed on April before she could finish her protest. I really didn't know why she was bothering. I was done with Christine for good.

On the top floor, ready to kick ass and take names, I marched purposefully to Christine's office and kicked her door open.

Seated at her desk with a man who looked vaguely familiar standing behind her, Christine jumped, startled by my brazen entry.

What the hell am I doing? I thought in a moment of panic.

"Victoria!" Christine barked with surprise. "What on earth do you think you're doing marching in here like that?"

"Shut up!" I snapped.

I can't believe I just said that, I thought, my heart pounding wildly within my chest.

Deafening silence descended upon the room, and the man standing behind Christine turned white with shock.

He probably thinks I'm crazy, talking to the queen of fashion like that, I thought, trying to quell my trembling limbs.

"Pierre, will you please allow me to deal with this . . . problem," Christine said quietly after a stunned moment.

"Certainly." He bowed his head with respect to Christine and walked out of the room, shaking his head as he passed me.

Christine centered her burning eyes on me like a hawk. "What did you just say to me, young lady?"

"I said shut up," I repeated.

"Do you realize who you're talking to?"

I giggled, fighting the tremors of anxiety rolling through my legs. Despite my anxiousness, I felt powerful. I was finally going to be free, and it felt good to be able to tell the witch what I'd been wanting to say since my first day on the job. "Sure I do. An unbearable, miserable, narcissistic, old hag who is so unhappy with her dull life that she makes a career out of giving young girls poor self-esteem issues."

"How dare you!" Christine raged, jumping to her feet

and gripping the edges of her desk with rage, her eyes blazing.

"How dare I?" I demanded, my body shaking from head to toe now. "How dare you! You've treated me like shit since I first started working for you and made my life a total hell. You know, at first I thought it was worth it. I thought that, hmmm, maybe working for this vile, evil woman would open doors for me one day, and I'll only have to suffer for a little while before I can find my own way. But you know what? Eat shit! Because it's not worth putting up with it anymore. I quit!"

The look of utter shock on Christine's face made my day and I let out a burst of maniacal laughter that I'm sure made Christine think I'd gone stark-raving mad.

This time, I didn't laugh as long as I had with April, and when I was done, I turned to leave but stopped to add, "Oh and by the way, you can save your little threats about how you will ruin me and how I will never work in this city again."

I flashed one last triumphant smile the witch's way and swirled around and began to leave the office. But the sound of Christine's voice brought me up short a second later.

"Victoria."

I should've ignored her and kept going. After all, I'd gotten the last word in, and there was no reason to engage her further and listen to her empty threats about how she would ruin me, but for some reason, the tone in her voice made me freeze. I *had* to hear what she was going to say.

Slowly, I turned around to see Christine regarding me with amusement in her eyes.

Why is she smiling? I wondered. *I just told her off. She should be steaming mad and wanting to kick my ass out of her office.*

"Do you recall when you first came to work for me?"

"Yeah? It was on a day that—"

She interrupted me, obviously not looking for me to actually answer her question. "You signed a contract."

Her words were like a sucker punch to the stomach.

I licked my lips that had suddenly gone as dry as a desert. "So? What does that matter?"

Now it looked like Christine was the one holding back maniacal laughter. "Do you recall what was in the contract, Miss Young?"

The room began to spin around me as panic began to seep in.

I'd been so desperate to get the job working for Christine, I hadn't thought to go read through it all, eager to sign my soul away for the chance at a future career in fashion. A chance at reaching that first step in achieving my dreams.

"No," I admitted.

Christine grinned. "The terms and conditions were that you cannot terminate your job with me without at least a sixty-day notice for any reason outside of a medical or family emergency without opening yourself to legal ramifications."

It took a lot to steady myself. Any second and I was going to faint.

Christine looked me over while speaking with glee. "And since the only emergency it looks like you're in is a dire need to lose another twenty pounds off your enormous rear end . . ." Christine's smile took over her entire face. "I could sue your fat ass off."

It was all I could do to stay standing. "Y-y-you can't do

that," I stammered.

Christine crossed her arms across her chest. "Watch me."

"That's not legal. Besides, it's not like I actually *have* anything to sue for."

Christine uncrossed her arms and leaned forward across her desk, boring into me with suddenly cold, calculating eyes. "Do you really want to take that chance with me, Victoria?"

When I didn't reply, Christine let out a chuckle, a heartless, evil sound that felt like a knife was being jabbed in my side. "I didn't think so." She snapped her fingers and did her customary 'shoo the fly' gesture. "Now go make my coffee."

* * *

"She's just doing this to keep me chained here!" I sobbed into my hands. "She's too sadistic to let me out of my contract and pursue my own career elsewhere."

"I'm sorry, Vick," April cooed, "but you should've known better than to try Christine. In fact, I'm in shock that you're still here. Telling Christine to shut up and calling her a miserable hag?" April shook her head and let loose a chuckle of disbelief. "No one has ever dared to say anything like that to her before . . . at least no one who has lived to tell the story, that is."

I sniffed, taking the back of my hand and wiping at my tears.

April and I were sitting at a small table. I had an untouched bagel with cream cheese on it while April had one celery stick. I don't know why she bothered. She might as well have had a plate of cotton balls in front of her for all the calories it contained.

News of my insubordination had spread like wildfire. I'd

had people casting furtive glances my way and whispering to each other. I knew what they were probably saying. Something along the lines of, *Did you hear about what Victoria said to Christine? She must have been born with a set of balls.*

"I know, right? I should be gone. If anyone else had said what I said, they'd have been fired in a New York minute. But me? She threatens to sue me to keep me working for her. It just goes to show how much she delights in my misery." I shook my head angrily. "She hates the fact that I'll be able to make a career for myself without her help."

"Will you though?" asked April skeptically.

I sniffed and then stared at her. "Will I what?"

"Be able to make a career for yourself? You still have a lot to learn, Vicky."

"Yeah." I paused. "Tyler said that he would help me in any way he can." I quickly outlined Tyler's offer to help me fund my career and maybe start a business together.

April studied me for a long moment before speaking. "You know I love you, Vick, but I'm sorry. Do you honestly believe this guy? You seriously can't be that naïve, Vick. The dude's a major player. He probably tells girls stuff like that all the time just to get them in bed."

"No, it's not like that, April," I hissed irritably, surprised at the anger dripping in my voice. I paused for a moment, sucking in a deep breath to calm myself before continuing. "At first I was like you, thinking he was a big time player, but I've since found out that he's not like that at all. He's got another side to him."

Who am I trying to convince? April or myself?

"I hope you're right, Vicky." April really didn't believe me, and a small part of me wondered if I didn't believe it myself. "But wait . . . didn't you find out that the guy is like your stepbrother or something?"

I shrugged. "Yeah? So?"

"So? Isn't that like kind of . . ."

I rolled my eyes at her insinuation. "Oh please, we're not related. Heck, we were total strangers until not so long ago."

"I guess you're right on that," April conceded after a moment of thought. "But either way, it's still going to make everything even more difficult. Besides, Vick, Christine owns your soul." Her eyes seemed to say to me what she wouldn't say, *maybe it's for the best.*

"But that's the thing . . . maybe I can get out of my contract."

April shook her head, taking a quick nibble on her celery stick. "Are you kidding me? Christine has like an army of lawyers. You'd never get out of it. I don't care what Tyler is telling you. Once he knows you're that much of liability, he'd drop you like a hot potato."

"You think so?"

April nodded. "I know so."

"Hey bitches!" chirped a familiar voice. Gabe came walking up to our table with a tray of food. Unlike April, he actually had food on his plate, a big fat hot dog and a side of fries. Gabe was as skinny as a rail, but he could eat as much as he wanted without getting fat. It was so unfair. So, so unfair.

Animated as a cartoon, Gabe sat his tray down on the table and then took his seat. "Hey Vick, you're like my fucking bitch of the hour! I hear you totally told Christine off."

I held in a groan. I really didn't feel like talking about anything right then, least of all my confrontation with Christine. "You heard right."

"Hell yeah!" Gabe picked up his hot dog and took a huge bite out of it before asking me his next question with a mouthful of food. "Tell me exactly how it went down. I want all the details!"

I shook my head and picked up my bagel, only to find my stomach turning. I had absolutely no appetite.

"You don't wanna know."

Chapter 13
Tyler

After Victoria had left, I'd taken a hot shower and started getting ready for work. I was buttoning my last cuff when Jonathan appeared at the top of the stairs.

"Is there something wrong, Master Locklin?"

I turned away from the mirror to regard the older man with irritation, who was peering at me with a look of concern. "What did I tell you about calling me Master, Jonathan?" I demanded. "It makes me sound like a damn slave owner."

I turned back to the mirror and rolled my shoulders, examining my appearance. There was a sparkle in my eye and a glowing flush to my skin. I knew I was handsome, but there was something more going on here. I looked . . . alive. More alive than I could ever remember.

It's Victoria, a voice in the back of my mind said. *She's done this to me.* It was scary, the way she made me feel. Even scarier, the way she made me lose control of rational thought.

What was I thinking, offering her something like that?

What the hell did I know about fashion? Better yet, I don't even really know what *she* knows. How could I offer to fund such a thing? I was supposed to be a damned businessman.

I'll just explain to her later that I didn't really mean what I said, I thought. *Much later.*

"I'm sorry Mast-, umm, Tyler," Jonathan replied,

breaking me out of my reverie. "It's a terrible habit, I suppose. Call me old-fashioned."

"Well get with the times. This isn't the 1800s anymore."

"You're right, sir. I'll try to be more thoughtful of that in the future." He paused. "Will we be taking the customary drive to Armex headquarters?"

I shook my head, turning away from the mirror and walking over to the bed to shoulder on my business coat. "No. I want to head by the Locklin estate. I'd like to pay my father a little visit."

* * *

"I trust your relationship with Victoria is over," my dad said as I stood before his desk in his study. A steaming coffee mug was before him, right beside the morning newspaper he routinely read before being chauffeured off to his office at Armex.

I did my best to hide my grin. "No. As a matter of fact, it's not."

Dad's head snapped up sharply. "What did you say?"

"Our relationship, it's not over. It's only just begun."

He pushed the paper across his desk and narrowed his eyes at me. I could tell he was pissed off, though he was doing his best to hide it.

"I warned you what would happen if you didn't break this thing off, Tyler," he growled.

"I know," I said in an offhand manner that I knew would make him want to jump my shit.

His jaw bulged, a sign that I'd indeed gotten to him this time. "So why are you still with her? She's your stepsister." He continued, his voice raising a few octaves. "Do you have any idea what kind of image problems this relationship will cause for Armex?"

I chuckled. "You know what? You're hilarious. First you badger the fuck out of me about settling down. Then, when I finally do find a girl to settle down with, she's not good enough for you."

"That's not true and you know it, Tyler," Dad growled. "You know very well why I don't approve of this relationship." He snorted with contempt. "If you can even call it that. And by the way, you haven't fooled me one bit. I still don't believe that you're willing to settle down. You want to know what I think?"

I crossed my arms. "You're going to tell me anyway, so go ahead."

"I think you got scared shitless when I threatened to replace you with Charles Whitmore, so you hastily latched onto the first girl you could find to put up with your bullshit to show me you'd changed." He scowled. "Well, you can drop the act now, Tyler. As long as you end this farce of a relationship and continue to behave, you're in no danger of losing your position with our company."

I hated to admit it, but for the first time since entering the room, I was pissed. My father was implying that I was scared of him and his threats when the truth was, I wasn't afraid of any fucking body. "Is that what you honestly think? You think that my relationship with Victoria is a farce?"

Dad gave me a puzzled expression. "It is, isn't it?"

"No!" I said sternly with my most convincing voice.

My dad stared at me for a few moments before a

surprised look took over his face as it dawned on him. "You're telling the truth, aren't you? There really is something between you two. I must admit, Tyler, I'm shocked."

I swallowed, feeling a heavy sensation pressing against my chest. I hated it. I hated how Victoria made me feel . . . like I was in . . .

*I can hardly even think those words. I even promised her help with her caree*r, I thought, *when I don't even know if I'd be able to keep my word.*

Hiring her was one thing; that I *could* do. But promising that I'd help her start a fashion business? What the fuck was I thinking?

I wasn't thinking, that's the problem, I thought. *My mind was mush. I'd have said anything if it meant I'd be able to fuck her again.*

There was something about being with Victoria that fucked with me.

She's dangerous, a voice in the back of my mind warned. *She could ruin you.* Not that I wasn't well on my way to doing that myself.

My dad's voice broke me out of my reverie as I pushed the unwanted voice out of my thoughts.

"Well, Tyler?"

"Look," I growled. "We aren't related. I really don't see the big deal here."

Dad stared. "You're not stupid Tyler, but let me spell it out for you. It's not that big of a deal, you're right. But you know how the media spins things."

"Who cares what these people think, Dad? Maybe they shouldn't live their lives judging others and mind their own damn business."

He took a deep breath, gathering himself. "Maybe in another time and place I'd agree with you, Ty, but these people that you need to please are not just regular old people. They're our customers, or potential customers. The very people that allow you to live the lifestyle that you do. You do care about that, don't you?" He shook his head. "I don't even see why I have to point this out to you. You know better. You know that our competitors will have a field day with this."

"Well it's too late now, Dad. What's done is done, and this isn't just any old relationship that I can just end . . ."

"Well, son, I think you're going to have to make a decision. Victoria or your position at Armex."

"That's such bullshit! I'm not breaking up with her," I declared defiantly.

"Tyler-"

"In fact," I said loudly, speaking over him, "I'm going to hire her, even if it is short-lived. So not only will you be firing your son, but your stepdaughter too!"

* * *

"That's just five," Jeff said as he leaned back in his seat across from me. I'd summoned my fellow colleague to my office for a little a private chat about what to do about the soon-to-come vote for my removal. He was enjoying a cheeseburger with bacon and fries from Wendy's while I dined on a grilled chicken sandwich. "You need at least six."

"Damn," I muttered.

"It's that God damn Charles Whitmore," Jeff growled, grabbing his Coke and taking a sip before setting it back down.

"If it weren't for him, you'd be in the clear."

"Fuck that dude."

"Yeah." Jeff swallowed and then stared at me. "But why go through all this trouble anyway? Why not just do what your father asked? Your stepsister can't be worth all this trouble, can she?"

"She's worth every bit of it, Jeff," I said firmly.

"I can't believe I'm hearing this. A few months ago, there was no chick on planet Earth that was worthy of your affection." Jeff finished off the rest of his cheeseburger and then shook. "I can't imagine it, though."

"Imagine what?"

"Banging my own stepsister."

I grinned. He caught me off guard on that one.

"Anyway," I said, abruptly changing the subject, "Who's on the fence in all this? All we have to do is get one of them to side with me."

Jeff picked up a napkin and wiped his hands before dropping it in the Wendy's bag. Grabbing a fry and then dipping it in ketchup, he sat back in his seat and leveled a serious gaze on me. "Well, there's Ritchie and Kevin."

"What about them?"

Jeff waved his red-tipped fry at my face. "Well, Rich wants an apology and he might consider voting in your favor. He doesn't like you, but if he had a chance to stick it to Charles, he'd take it."

I snorted. "An apology? For what?"

Jeff popped the French fry in his mouth and chewed. "For sleeping with his ex."

"Seriously?"

Jeff nodded. "Her name is Mandy Lane, remember her?"

I racked my brain for the girl's face, but I couldn't come up with an image. "No," I said finally. "I don't."

Jeff grabbed another fry and waved it theatrically. "That's unfortunate. Very unfortunate."

"Yeah, even more unfortunate because I'm not apologizing. From what you said, he wasn't even with her anymore. Why does he even care?"

"Oh come on, Ty. You know how it is, he was hoping to rekindle things."

"Look, just forget all this scheming. Whatever happens, will happen. If my dad wants to help remove me, then so be it."

The truth was that my pride would never let me grovel, even if it meant keeping my job. It was just one of my pitfalls as a man. My pride always got in the way.

Shaking his head, Jeff popped his fry into his mouth, smacked his hands together several times to rid himself of salt and then stood up. "Well, it's your decision, buddy. I'd hate to be in your position," he warned as he grabbed his leftover fries and dumped them into his Wendy's bag as he prepared to leave my office. "It's your future on the line, after all."

Chapter 14

Victoria

"I can't come work for you," I said, holding back tears. I was sitting beside Tyler, who'd shown up at the end of my shift in his limo after a long, arduous day at work.

Tyler looked at me, making my heart flip.

My God, I can't get enough of him, I thought. It never ceased to amaze me how the man could just turn me into mush with one simple look.

"Why not?"

He seems to be taking this news well, I thought, searching his face for disappointment. I saw none. For some reason, that bothered me.

Holding back my crocodile tears, I explained what happened when I'd confronted Christine. "She doesn't want me to work for anyone else," I said as I finished my tale. "She revels in my misery."

"What a sadistic cunt," growled Tyler.

He still wasn't breaking down in tears. Not that I'd expected that, but I was hoping for a little more disappointment at least.

"Tell me about it," I muttered. "I felt like such an idiot when I remembered my contract. I should've known I'd forgotten something."

"Don't beat yourself up over it," Tyler soothed. "You

were in the heat of the moment. You couldn't have known."

But you should be more upset about this, I thought. *You seemed so excited this morning, but now you seem . . . subdued.* It pissed me off that I didn't have the courage to come right out and tell him that.

The cabin fell silent as our driver, Jonathan, rolled to a stop at a stoplight.

"So what are we going to do?" I asked a moment later. "I must admit, I was totally looking forward to working with you." I flashed a nervous smile at him. "And then later on, maybe be your partner."

Tyler hesitated, and for a second I saw indecision flicker in his eyes.

Is he having second thoughts? I wondered. I hated that about myself. I'm a pretty headstrong girl most of the time, but I do have my insecurity issues too. The thought bothered me more than I wanted to admit. It meant that I'd been a fool all along.

When Tyler didn't respond right away, I shifted in my seat, feeling an almost overwhelming panic take control of my limbs. "Are you okay?" I asked, trying my hardest to keep my voice level and firm.

Tyler coughed and shook his head. "Uh, yeah. I was just thinking."

"About what?" my voice cracked.

Damnit. Another moment longer and I was sure I'd burst into tears. *If that happens,* I thought, *I'm jumping out at the next stop light and never looking back.*

Tyler finally seemed to sense my anxiety and wrapped a consoling arm over my shoulder. "Don't worry, babe. I think I know who can help."

"Who?" I wondered, trying not to cry.

"Brad, a lawyer friend of mine," Tyler replied confidently. "I had a meeting planned with him at Bixby's diner tomorrow during lunch."

"Bixby's," I muttered. I thought I'd heard of that one, a trendy restaurant near Christine's. It was a little upscale and out of my league.

"Yeah. Anyway, we were going to go over the legal options I have if I'm removed. How about you stop by on your lunch break tomorrow? We'll talk to him about it, see if there's anything you can do to get out of it. If not, we'll just have to wait."

"He'd do that?" I asked, swallowing back the lump in my throat. Just Tyler having his arm around me was doing a lot to calm my nerves. The man was out of this world. He could make me suspicious of him, doubt myself, and love him all at once.

Tyler chuckled. "Yeah. He owes me big time."

"For what?"

Tyler grinned. "You remember where we first met?"

I rolled my eyes. "How could I forget?" Images of Tyler's chiseled thighs and enormous bulge flashed in front of my eyes, making the heat rise within my body.

Your lips would look good wrapped around my . . .

"Well those guests you guys were fitting were for Brad's wedding, and guess who's footing the bill?"

"Okay," I said, smiling. It was nice to know that Tyler would do that for someone, even if it was a drop in the bucket for him.

Tyler planted a kiss on my cheek. "Everything will be all right, baby."

My breath quickened at his words and his hand that was now on my thigh.

"What are you doing?" I demanded

Tyler's beautiful eyes sparkled with mischief. "You left me hanging this morning. I'm just getting what I've been waiting for all day."

I glanced uneasily up at the front of the limo. There was a glass window separating us and Jonathan, but I wasn't sure if he could see through it.

"In here? While he's driving?"

My breath quickened as Tyler's eyes bore into me with an intensity that made my thighs quiver like Jell-O.

Tyler pushed my legs open wide and winked at me, giving me a grin that said, *I'm about to fuck you and you're going to love it.* Who could resist?

* * *

The next day, after a grueling morning with Christine, who'd sent me around the building like a chicken with my head cut off, running errand after impossible errand, I stopped by Bixby's to meet up with Tyler and his friend, Brad, to have lunch.

After the hot session I'd been treated to in the back of Tyler's limo, I was anxious to see my beautiful boyfriend again and to meet his childhood best friend. Tyler seemed to limit those he called friends, and I was curious to see what he was like.

"Looks like you're in a bit of a pickle," Brad announced,

closing the last page of the form and sliding it across the smooth, marble table to me. "She's right. I'd recommend going ahead and giving your notice."

Though not as handsome as Tyler, Brad was a very attractive guy. When I'd arrived at the restaurant, he greeted me like the utmost gentleman, pulling out my seat and giving my hand a kiss, which had prompted a jealous warning from Tyler. The two began bickering back and forth over it, and I thought for a minute that they'd come to blows when I finally realized that they were just playing.

After that playful introduction, we sat down to figure out our orders. It wasn't long after our food came that we got down to business and I'd given Brad my contract to look over.

My heart fell into my chest as I took the form and slid it back into my purse.

So much for that, I thought with disappointment.

Despite knowing how badly I wanted out of my contract, Tyler didn't seem too bothered by it. *Here I go again*, I thought as the familiar feelings of suspicion began to creep back in. I did my best to dismiss the feelings.

"That's pretty much your only option," Brad said, picking up his knife and slicing into the premium steak he'd ordered.

"I guess I'll go ahead and give her notice then," I said slowly.

Beside me, Tyler became quiet, arousing my suspicions further.

My heart pounded within my chest as I was overcome with a volley of emotions. The worse part of it all was the look in Tyler's eyes. It was one of indecision.

It's not all in my head, after all.

I wanted to accuse him of going back on his word, and I almost did, but I didn't want to start an argument in front of Brad, who'd been nothing but polite to me.

Right then, the waitress came up, a blonde with a bad dye job.

"Is everything going alright?" she purred, moving closer to Tyler than I was comfortable with.

"Fine, thanks," Brad said shortly, flashing her a boyish grin.

"I'd like another glass, please," Tyler asked politely.

The waitress grinned as if he'd offered her a night of hot sex. "Coming right up, handsome," she giggled, playfully clapping him on the shoulder.

Tyler grinned back at her, his eyes sparkling.

That was more than I could take. The only thing that kept me from jumping up from my seat and dragging Miss-Bad-Dye-Job across the restaurant was the fact that I didn't want to embarrass myself in front of Tyler's friend.

"I have to go," I announced suddenly as soon as the waitress sashayed off. I jumped up from my seat, trying unsuccessfully to keep my limps from trembling.

Tyler started to get up from his seat, but I quickly motioned him back down. "Already?"

I have to go to keep from going into a rage and embarrassing us both in front of your best friend.

"Yeah. Christine needed me to schedule a very important upcoming show for her as soon as I got back from lunch." I flashed a fraudulent smile at Brad. "It was nice meeting you, Brad. Thank you so much for your counsel, and I hope your wedding is one to remember."

Brad smiled back and nodded his head at me. "It was no problem, and it was nice meeting you too. You have a nice day."

"I will." I tossed a quick glance at Tyler, trying to keep a straight face. "Thanks for the meal." I turned and began walking away from the table.

"What? I don't get a kiss?" I heard Tyler call behind me.

I ignored his question and kept walking out of the restaurant, grateful that he couldn't see the tears of frustration rolling down my face. My emotions were on a roller coaster, and I needed to get out of the situation before I did something I'd regret.

Tyler

I immediately resisted the urge to jump up and follow Victoria out of the restaurant.

I'll just end up making things worse if I go after her, I thought, angry that I hadn't been able to hide the fact that I was having second thoughts about our future business venture.

Telling her how I felt after her jealous reaction would only result in her feeling like she'd been right all along: I was a manwhore who'd say or do anything to get into the next girl's pants.

"Geez," Brad said over a mouthful of steak. "She seemed

extra pissed when the waitress flirted with you."

"She was," I muttered, glancing down at my food. My stomach turned at the sight and I put down my fork. I'd lost my appetite.

"Damn, this steak is as tough as a donkey's ass. With what this place charges, you would think you'd get better." Brad gave me a look as he chewed. "How are you two going to last if she gets mad at that? Chicks hitting on you is an everyday occurrence."

"Her confidence is a little shook up with all the stuff that's been going down, that's all. She's normally pretty feisty. Anyway, I don't think that's what she was really upset at, though it didn't help."

Braid raised an eyebrow. "What else then?"

I didn't respond, because Miss Flirty Pants came over to see if we needed anything.

"No thanks," I said. "We're fine." I avoided eye contact with her.

"So tell me what's going on. You're not getting away that easily." Brad pressed.

"I really don't want to talk about it. I'm pissed enough at myself about it already."

Brad paused for a moment and wiped around his mouth with a napkin. "Come on, man. Maybe I can help."

I knew if I didn't tell him, he'd just keep bugging the shit out of me. "Okay, fine." I sighed. I quickly outlined to him what I'd promised Victoria.

Brad let out a low whistle when I was finished. "Man, I can't believe it."

"Believe what?" I asked, knowing that I was falling into a trap.

"This chick has got you whipped."

"Oh shut the fuck up. And hey, I'm not the one getting married."

"Yeah, but I never swore off serious relationships either. I mean, after Candice—"

"Can you not mention her name?" I snapped.

Brad managed to look guilty "Sorry. I didn't mean to bring her up. I know that one's a tough subject."

"I'm sure you didn't," I said sarcastically. "But really, I know what you mean. I didn't think I'd ever get back into a real relationship either. But Victoria . . ." I shook my head, looking for the words. "She's just different. She's beautiful, smart, headstrong, knows what she wants and—"

"She's your stepsister."

"Exactly."

"I guess that does add a little excitement to it."

Brad took a swig from his wineglass and shook his head. "This is some crazy shit. The one girl that you finally decide that you actually want to be with winds up being your stepsister. I can't believe your luck."

I shrugged. "Stranger things have happened."

"Ain't that the fucking truth." Brad set his wine down and his expression turned serious. "But . . . I gotta ask, and don't get pissed . . . is she really worth it? I mean, is it worth losing your job over her?"

My immediate impulse was to snap at Brad's suggestion, but I resisted. The truth was, I didn't know what anything was

107

anymore. I wasn't used to dealing with this kind of emotion, and it was messing with my head.

I don't know how to feel or to think, I thought. *I swore I would never be in this position again, worrying about another female and fulfilling her wants, needs and desires, only to be betrayed by her in the end. Yet, here I am, trying to figure out how I can keep my job and keep her all at the same time. And for what?*

It was scary, the feelings that Victoria evoked in me. She made me want to be a better man. She made me want to treat her with the respect that she deserved, made me want to be her knight in shining armor. For anyone else, it would have been a godsend. But for me, it was all new, and it both scared me and pissed me off at the same time.

I've got to do something about this, I thought. *I can't keep on like this—wanting her but too afraid of being with her.*

"Anyway," I said, changing the subject because I didn't want to talk about it anymore until I actually had it sorted in my head. "I'm calling my dad's bluff. I still have my doubts he'll go through with it, but if he does call a vote to remove me, I want to know my options."

Brad sat back in his chair and pushed his half-eaten steak away from him. "Well you have a couple of options, but only two make sense."

"You can fight it in court, but . . ." Brad scratched at the stubble on his jaw, reluctant to continue. After a moment, he sighed and said, "The fact is, to be completely honest with you, Ty, I'm not looking forward to that. It's just a lose-lose scenario all around. Not to mention with the wedding coming up and Katie's constant demands to make everything as perfect as possible, the stress of a drawn-out court case will probably put me in an early grave. So that basically leaves you with two options."

"And what are those?" I asked, curious.

"The first, and I'm just putting it out there, is to end your relationship with Victoria. I know it's not what you wanted to hear, but that's option one."

I couldn't help myself. "Well aren't you just fucking useless."

"I know, I know, I said it's not what you wanted to hear, but it had to be said. Look, you're not going to like option two either, but if your feelings for Victoria are real, it has to be done."

I gave him one of those *Did I just smell a fart?* puzzled looks.

"You need to have a heart-to-heart with your father."

Chapter 15
Victoria

The following day on lunch hour, I was sitting at my desk eating a donut. A big, powdered, jelly-filled donut. And I never, ever ate donuts. I was always too worried about gaining a pound. It definitely felt good now, but I'd regret it later. Damn Christine and her giving me self-esteem issues.

But today she could kiss my ass. I didn't give a damn if I gained a pound, because my relationship with Tyler was on the rocks and I was super fucking depressed.

After I left Bixby's, the image of him smiling at the waitress kept flashing in my head, filling me with rage and hurt. At least, that's what I told myself. In all honesty, I think I was just looking for another reason to be mad. He'd really let me down with his nonchalant attitude.

I should've known he was no good. He just saw me as an interesting conquest. After he got what he wanted from me, I was no longer a priority. All that talk that he would fight our parents on my behalf? Obviously bullshit. He's just a stubborn asshole that wants to defy authority. That, and he just wanted to make a point to his father that he can do what he wants.

The worst part of it all was that I'd totally humiliated myself and nearly destroyed my career, all on the basis of Tyler's false promises.

I'm lucky to still be working, I thought angrily. Thankfully,

Christine's ever-present need to torture me was the only reason I still had a job. I'd come so close to losing everything, all because I lost all rational thought when I was around Tyler. The image in my mind absolutely frightened me.

I definitely dodged a bullet with that one.

A ringing sound caused me to jump. My desk phone.

It's him! I thought angrily, nearly choking on a mouthful of jelly donut. *It's that womanizing jerk.*

Really, I had no clue if it was him calling, but I convinced myself that it was.

Don't answer it.

I knew I shouldn't have. I'd ignored his calls to my cell all day. But for some reason, I couldn't help myself. I wanted to let him know that I was pissed off.

I quickly swallowed the rest of my donut, and after a deep breath, I snatched the phone.

I filled my voice with the nastiest venom I could muster. "I don't want to speak to you ever again!"

"Victoria!" my mother's voice snapped.

"Mom," I breathed in shock. At this time in my life, my mother was the last person on earth I wanted to have a conversation with. "What do you want, Mother?"

Her voice rose several octaves. "What do I want? What do I want?! Do you have any idea how much shame you've put on this family or how much trouble you've caused for me?"

"Seriously, Mom? We haven't spoken in ages, and this is what you choose to call me about? Like, how was I supposed to know that you were married to Tyler's father? We don't even talk!"

She acted as if she didn't even hear me. "You've caused me so much embarrassment, Victoria."

"You'll be happy to know that Tyler and I are finished," I cut in, not willing to listen to any more of my mother's crap. "He's a womanizing asshole, so you'd better watch out for James. It probably runs in the family."

I slammed down the phone.

"The nerve of that woman," I muttered angrily. How she got a billionaire to ever marry her, I would never know.

"Victoria!" Christine called from her office. "Get in here. NOW." There was no doubt about it, the witch meant business.

I held in a sigh as I quickly brushed the donut crumbs off of my desk and prepared to go face Christine and muttered, "my life is over."

Tyler

I should call it off, I thought to myself as I was riding home from work. *End it right now and cut my losses.*

The way Victoria left the restaurant and had been ignoring my calls said that she was probably considering the same thing.

It'd be for the best, I tried to tell myself. *I can't even think around her. She drives me crazy with lust. I can't have that. Since Candice, I've always been in control.*

The fact that I'd sacrifice my position at my own company for a girl I'd only known for a short while? It was insane. My pride was one thing. I hated being told what to do by anyone. It'd always been one of my faults and I'd learned to accept that. But knowing you were fighting a losing battle and continuing to fight anyway—that was plain stupid.

It appeared that Brad wasn't too keen on any legal battle, and if I put my pride aside, neither was I.

I thought about Brad and the options he laid out for me. *Maybe I should just cave in to my dad's demands*, I thought. *Let Victoria go and pretend to be what my father wants me to be.*

The thought hurt as a sharp pain lanced through my chest. Even the *thought* of leaving Victoria hurt. I hated it. Fucking hated it. She made me feel weak.

I suddenly had the overpowering urge to see her, to make things right. Feeling that I was making a big mistake, I dug out my cell and speed-dialed her number.

No answer.

It had been the same thing all day.

If I wanted to get a hold of her, I was going to have to be a bit more direct.

"Jonathan," I called to the front of the limo.

"Yes, Master Locklin?"

I ignored his mistake of calling me master again, my mind on Victoria.

"Turn this thing around and take me downtown. There's someone I need to see."

Victoria

"Finally the day is over," I muttered in relief as I grabbed

113

my things. I couldn't wait to go home to my rat hole of an apartment and kick back. My feet were killing me. Walking around in 3-inch heels all day will do that to you.

Too bad I won't have Tyler to rub them for me, I thought sourly. *Or have the luxury of relaxing in his loft.*

Though I wasn't superficial by any means, that was definitely something I'd miss . . . his beautiful loft, being chauffeured around in a limo, the wining and the dining.

Johnathan was right. Walking out the door and never coming back again would've been the best thing I could've ever done for myself. I was just too blind to see it until now.

The problem was that my feelings didn't quite align with what I was trying to tell myself. I felt like I was under a black cloud that was stealing all my sunshine.

"It will pass," I muttered to myself. "Before long, I'll forget a Tyler Locklin ever existed."

After making sure everything in Christine's office was in order, I made my way outside the building.

I'd only gotten two steps out of the front door when a familiar Limo pulled up.

Oh no.

I started to turn away and walk as fast as my sore feet could carry me, but the back door swung open and I went weak in the knees at the sight of Tyler climbing out.

He was dressed in his normal business attire, the outfit most likely costing more than my rent. He had a determined look about him. Even though I was angry as hell, I had to admit—he looked sexy. Fucking hot.

Run, I urged myself. *Run and don't look back.* But I couldn't move. My feet were rooted in place.

"Hey," Tyler greeted me.

I let out an explosive breath. I was so captivated by the image of him that I'd forgotten to breathe.

"What are you doing here?" I demanded, trying to sound as bitchy as possible but failing. "I don't want to talk to you."

Even with it being dusk out, I could see the ever-mischievous sparkle in Tyler's eyes. "You sure about that?"

"Yes, I'm sure. Get lost," I said, but my words didn't sound convincing at all.

Tyler chuckled and then his expression became serious just as fast. He gestured at the limo. "Get in," he growled, his deep voice filling me with dread and excitement all at once.

I hesitated for a moment, my mind filled with turmoil. *You can still walk away.*

"Now!" He added. "We need to talk." My body tingled at the sexy, guttural sound that seemed to promise retribution and pleasure all at once.

Before I knew it, I was moving past him and into the limo, thinking to myself, *I'm making a big mistake.*

Chapter 16
Victoria

"So this is *your* office?" I asked in disbelief.

Tyler had brought me to his office, nestled on the top floor of the Armex headquarters. The view, which had wall-long windows, was absolutely spectacular. The skyline twinkled in the background, crowded with hi-rise buildings.

In the middle of the room sat a large, cherry wood desk and a giant-sized leather chair that looked inviting. The chair almost reminded me of a throne.

Made for a King.

The whole room had a luxurious feel. Swanky and high class. *I could learn to love working in a place like this*, I thought.

The little office Christine had me working in was a dilapidated hovel compared to the splendor before me. Tyler stuck both hands in his pocket and grinned, amused by my awe. "You like it, don't you?"

I walked over to the glass window and peered out at the breathtaking skyline. "How could I not? It's stunning."

"I'm glad you do. It's the best view in the entire building." His intense gaze made goosebumps rise on my skin. I averted my eyes back to the skyline.

"This is beautiful,' I breathed.

"Not as beautiful as you."

I rolled my eyes. "Stop it."

"Don't bait me then."

That wasn't my intention in the least. "I wasn't baiting you."

God, he makes me want to kill him, I thought, *and **screw** him at the same time.*

I turned away from the window and crossed my arms. "I bet you thought that two-bit waitress at Bixby's was beautiful too."

Tyler sighed. "Come on. Why are you acting so pissed about that? It was nothing."

"So did you and Brad find a resolution to our—your problem?" I asked, changing the subject. I didn't want to keep talking about the waitress. He was right, it was nothing.

Tyler shook his head. "No. In fact, he was pretty useless." A shadow passed over his face. "Let's not talk about that right now."

"Well, I've decided not to put in my notice with Christine," I announced suddenly as I watched for Tyler's reaction.

He was silent for a moment.

"Why?" he asked finally.

I walked away from the window and circled his office, eyeing all the exquisite details before stopping at the side of his desk. "Because I realize that I'd probably be making a very big mistake. I'm lucky that Christine didn't fire me. I still don't quite understand that one. If she had, who knows where I'd be?"

Tyler scowled. "You'd be lucky? You said she treats you like shit, remember?"

"I'd rather be treated like shit than to fall in love with a guy, only to find out that he'll cheat on me once he's bored and finds another desperate chick to warm his bed."

"Is that what you think will happen with us?"

"I *know* that's what will happen. Your past speaks for itself, and I ignored everyone's warning for far too long," I said firmly. I couldn't believe what I was saying, and it was hard to keep my legs from trembling. "In fact, I don't even know why I agreed to come here. You've all but told me with your body language that you're uncomfortable with me quitting my job and coming to work for you anyway."

Silence filled the room as we gazed at each other. Tyler made the first move, walking over to his chair and sitting down. He pushed himself back away from his desk, spreading his legs out wide.

The way he looked in that chair, so masculine and inviting, almost made me want to jump him right then and there. *He looks like . . . a boss. The fucking King of the World.*

He titled his head as he studied me, his eyes glittering. "I think you need some convincing."

My mouth was dry as I tried not to stare. He was really turning me on. "Convincing of what?"

"That I'm not what you think of me. That I'm serious when I say that I want to be with you."

I snorted. "Please."

"I'm fucking serious." Tyler motioned at me. "Come here."

"Are you crazy?" I demanded. "I'm not going anywhere near you." It pissed me off at how unconvincing I sounded, and it was hard not to tremble beneath his gaze.

"Fuck!" Tyler cried out randomly, grabbing at his sides, his face seemingly twisting with pain. Without thinking, I rushed around his desk to his side and placed my hands on his shoulder. "Are you okay—"

Tyler suddenly straightened in his seat and smiled up at me, his eyes sparkling. "Gotcha."

I swung my palm at his face, but he was quick to react, catching my wrist inches away from his cheek and pulling me into a hard, lingering kiss.

I broke away with a gasp, my chest heaving, my limbs trembling uncontrollably. "How dare you!"

Tyler smiled up at me, unperturbed by my faux rage. "Oh, I dare." He spread his legs out wider. "I dare you to have your way with me."

My heart pounded in my chest as I stared at the challenge in his eyes. The man was serious. He was challenging me to do whatever I wanted with him, however I wanted.

I should slap him, I thought, and I actually did it this time. I slapped him across the face. His head whipped to the side and he slowly turned his head back to face me, letting out a mocking chuckle.

"Is that the best you could do?"

I slapped him again, harder this time. I even managed to leave a red mark on his cheek.

Tyler was still unfazed by my efforts, laughing harder. "You hit like a bitch."

That's it!

I jumped into his lap, straddling him, and pulled his tie around his neck, choking him.

119

"Wanna' talk shit now?" I snarled in his face, choking him with his tie. "Not so funny now, huh, bad boy?"

Tyler ignored my best efforts, pulling me in for another kiss that left me dizzy and wheezing against his neck.

I smacked him for the third time, my breathing ragged. "I didn't say you could touch me!" I snapped, majorly turned on. Down below, I could feel his hard on pressing against me. It made me wet, wanton with desire.

I jumped out of his lap, my gaze furious. Tyler eyed me with amusement as I turned around and snatched open one of the drawers in his desk, looking for something I could use on him.

I dug through a couple of drawers until I found a spare tie he had tucked away. I quickly snatched the tie out and went around to the back of Tyler's chair. I grabbed his arms and pulled them behind the chair, tying his wrists together.

"What do you think you're doing?" Tyler asked. His voice was tinged with excitement, sending a thrill through my body.

"Just shut up and sit there."

Deftly, I undid his loose tie from around his throat and wrapped it around his eyes, blindfolding him.

"There," I muttered when I was finished, surveying my work.

Here was this sexy, handsome, powerful man sitting right in front of me, bound and tied. Ready for me to have my way with him. I wanted to jump him. Right then. Right there. And have glorious, hot and steamy sex. But that just wouldn't do. I needed to vent some frustration.

What are you doing, Victoria?

I ignored my annoying conscience and pushed Tyler out and away from his desk and into the middle of the room.

"You've been a very, very naughty boy, Mr. Locklin," I purred, circling Tyler's chair.

Tyler tilted his head to the side, trying to get a lock on my position. "I have?"

I didn't answer, and instead, stooped to take off my heels. I took one of them, a glittering red pump, and stepped in front of him. I gently pressed the stiletto into his chest and ran it down, ripping the fabric of his shirt.

"Uh, Victoria?" Tyler's normally confident voice sounded slightly nervous. "What are you doing?"

I giggled. "Punishing you."

"Well, shit, can you do that without ripping up my clothes? That shirt was five hundred bucks."

I grinned, though I knew he couldn't see my expression, grabbing a hold of either side of his shirt. I jerked as hard as I could, and a ripping sound filled the room as the material came apart in my hands, leaving him bare-chested.

"You're going to be sorry for that," Tyler growled.

I moved forward, grabbing him roughly by the hair, and tilted his head back so that his neck was exposed. I ran my tongue up his neck, watching his body shiver with anticipation, all the way to his ear and then whispered, "Didn't I tell you to shut the fuck up?"

Running my hands down his bare chest, I pressed my lips against his neck, kissing gently, repeatedly. Tyler's lips parted to let out a deep groan, the sound causing tingling within my nether regions.

My hands continued down his chest to latch onto his bulge. He was already rock hard and throbbing, straining against the expensive slacks, screaming to be let out. I could feel a soft moistness on my fingertips. His precum.

Messaging him through the soft material, I kissed up his neck to his lips, biting gently on his lower lip, sucking on it. I sunk my teeth into his flesh, pulling it back gently and then letting go.

"Shit," Tyler moaned. "That's fucking sexy—"

I darted my tongue into his mouth, interrupting him, and swirled it all around, enjoying the taste of him. As we tongued each other, his cock seemed to swell even more in my hands. By this time, my panties were soaked.

I suddenly wanted to taste him. I broke off our passionate kiss. He moaned in disappointment, his breathing ragged and heavy. Still holding onto his cock, I rose out of his lap and lowered myself to my knees.

His bulge was huge, making my mouth water and filling me with anticipation. Slowly, teasingly, I undid the belt. A second later, I had his pants down around his ankles, staring in amazement at what had brought me so much pleasure in days past. Precum oozed out of the tip, running down his long, thick shaft.

I moved in close, blowing on it gently. Tyler's whole body shivered. I lapped my tongue at the tip of his head like a kitten lapping at milk. He shuddered again.

"Oh God," he groaned. "That's not fucking fair." He struggled with his binding. "Untie me."

"I'll do no such thing," I growled, squeezing his cock for

122

his disobedience and watching more precum ooze out. "You dared me to do what I wanted to do with you, didn't you?"

"I did. But—"

"Well then shut up and let me vent my frustration!" I grinned. I was totally loving this.

"You're going to pay for this," Tyler warned.

I ignored him and stuffed his cock into my mouth, taking as much of the shaft down as I could. Tyler groaned, his whole body trembling. I went up and down, slurping and sucking while massaging his balls. I started to use both hands to stroke his long cock as I moved my mouth in tandem with my stroking. Slurping sounds filled my ears as the taste of sweet, masculine meat tickled the back of my throat.

"Oh, fuck me," Tyler groaned as I gobbled his cock like I was mining for come.

After a few more furious slurps, his shaft grew impossibly hard in my hands and his balls tightened, signaling he was ready. By now, his whole body was shaking, and his breathing was coming out in short gasps.

Payback time.

I pulled back, releasing him, his cock snapping back against his rock-hard abs with an audible thud.

"What the hell are you doing?" Tyler demanded, his voice strained and filled with panic. "I was about to blow my balls out."

I chuckled and rose to my feet. "Paying you back."

"Fuck this."

With a roar, Tyler tore out of his bindings with brute strength and jumped to his feet. His cock swayed to and fro, and he ripped the tie from around his eyes. His eyes cut into me like daggers, filled with wrath. I knew right then that I was in serious trouble.

Oh shit.

I tried to scramble away as fast as I could, but I didn't make it two steps. Tyler grabbed me roughly by the arms, spinning me out in front of him. The heat from his body enveloped me as he pressed into my back. Below, I could feel his hard, throbbing cock rubbing up against my ass.

"I told you, you were going to pay," he growled into my ear, his breath hot on my neck. I nearly swooned in his grasp, my body temperature rising to unbelievable levels.

"But you dared me to have my way with you," I protested in ragged little breaths.

"Fuck that," Tyler snarled. "You played dirty. Now it's my turn."

I had to admit, I wanted it badly. My whole body was burning, trembling with anticipation.

I couldn't believe how badly I wanted to feel Tyler's cock inside of me. More than ever before. I'd turned into a hungry cock whore, eager to please. It's true what they say, make up sex was the best sex.

"I was innocent before I met you," I whispered, wishing I had the strength to pull away, but I didn't. "You've completely corrupted me."

Tyler grinned. He knew he had me right where he wanted me. "I guess that makes me the devil."

Keeping my arms pinned together, he picked up one of the ties off the floor and quickly bound my hands behind my

124

back. Then he shoved me forward, bending me over his desk.

I let out a gasp as his powerful hands gripped my waist and then latched on to my skirt. In one powerful jerk, Tyler ripped it off, along with my panties. Next followed my shirt and bra. In an instant, cool air enveloped my naked body, sending goosebumps all over my ass and thighs, hardening my nipples.

I shivered in anticipation. Here I was, naked at the top of one of the most prominent corporate buildings in the city, being ogled by a gorgeous, rich stud.

Smack!

A sharp gasp escaped my lips and I winced.

Bastard!

"You like that?" I heard him growl behind me.

"Shit. You smack worse than I do," I hissed.

I regretted my words a moment later.

The next smack on my ass made me cry out, and I dug my nails into the hard wood of his desk to bear the pain. This one *hurt*, but it felt so *good* at the same time. I was sure Tyler had left a red print on my ass cheek.

Tyler laughed mockingly. "What'd I tell you? I don't hear you running that pretty little mouth of yours now."

Before I could reply, Tyler plunged two fingers inside me, causing me to gasp out again.

"You're going to learn that there will always be consequences," Tyler lectured as he probed my insides.

"I . . ." I gasped, pleasure rolling up through my stomach. "You're such a fucking bastard!"

"Oh yeah?"

"Yeah!" I cried, knowing I was asking for more trouble

but wanting it. I needed it. Suddenly, his tongue was lapping at me while his fingers still probed me.

"Oh," I moaned, digging my nails harder into the wood. I'm sure there would be scratch marks on it, but I didn't care.

His mouth enveloped my entire clit, sucking and slurping, still relentlessly thrusting into me with his two fingers. My ass jiggled on his face, and wet, wiggly noises filled the room as he scattered my juices everywhere.

"Oh fuck!" I cried.

There was only so much I could take. Fire raged through my stomach like molten lava, and I cried out as I came so hard, my thighs trembled like an earthquake.

The room spun around me as spasms of pleasure took over my body, and it was a moment before I regained consciousness of my surroundings. I came out of it, shaking and shivering, gasping and trying to recover. But oh no, Tyler wasn't having it. The bastard wasn't through with me.

He kept me bent over his desk as he rose to his feet. He waited for a few moments, teasing me with his cock, allowing me a couple of minutes to recover.

He entered me. Ruthlessly. I cried out as he penetrated me to what seemed like the entire length of my canal, and he began seesawing his giant cock in and out of me. As he pounded away, he grabbed me by the hair, pulling with enough force to make me wince. Garbled, unintelligible cries escaped my lips as I was viciously fucked.

It felt like a giant pole penetrating me. A fucking monster. His thrusts were *hard. Deep. Powerful.* And the smack of his powerful thighs hitting up against my ass filled the room.

Tyler made low, guttural growls of pleasure as he continued, taking my body for his own pleasure, owning every single particle of me. I dug into the desk, holding on for dear life. I'd never experienced sex this rough and intense, but it was absolutely amazing.

A couple of thrusts later, I could feel his cock stiffening inside me and his grip on my hair loosened as his breathing became heavy and labored, his thrusts slower but more full.

Oh shit. He doesn't have a condom on, I thought suddenly with alarm, remembering he hadn't put on protection, but being so caught up in the moment that I hadn't stopped him.

"Pull out," I gasped hoarsely. My words sounded garbled to my ears. "Tyler!" I tried to pull away, but I was firmly in his grasp, his hands holding onto my waist with a powerful grip.

At the very last second, he pulled out, roaring like a lion, and I could feel his hot come splash on my back and my ass.

I felt sore, inside and out. He'd really given me a pounding. I was sure I wouldn't be walking straight for a couple of days. "You could've come inside of me!"

It scared me how quickly our little power-play game had nearly spun out of control into something that we both could've possibly regretted.

"Relax," Tyler exhaled, sweat running down his jawline from his exertions. Though I was upset, I had to admit—Tyler was a glory to behold. His chest and abs glistened with sweat, his cock half-limp. He was the perfect male specimen. "I had it covered."

"Yeah, okay," I hissed sarcastically.

"What are you so worried about, aren't you on the pill?"

"Yeah, but still. That was fucking rude."

The feel of hot stickiness dripping down my backside left me looking around for something to wipe myself with. I grabbed his tie and put it to good use.

"Hey," Tyler protested as I wiped at my backside with his tie. "That tie is one of my favorites."

I casually tossed it onto his desk and bent down to retrieve my skirt off the floor. Tyler bent down to pick up his boxers, quickly slipping them on along with his slacks.

He grinned at me as he picked up his shirt, but his expression turned serious as he pulled it on, leaving it unbuttoned. "I've never done that before," he said quietly, gazing at me strangely.

I paused in pulling my half-ripped skirt up over my thighs to regard him. "Done what?"

"Been so reckless. "

I pulled my skirt all the way on and grabbed my bra, putting it on and snapping it back in place. "Then why'd you do it?" I asked softly.

"Because you make me so . . ." His voice trailed off, his eyes distant.

I stood there, hanging upon his every word. "I make you so what?"

Suddenly, his jaw hardened. "Never mind."

"Come on, tell me."

He shook his head, walking over to the door of his office while simultaneously buttoning up his shirt. "Get the rest of your clothes on and meet me outside. I'm taking you to my place to get cleaned up."

I opened my mouth to protest. After all, he didn't *ask* if I wanted to go back to his place, but he interrupted me.

"And make sure you grab that tie on your way out, will you? I don't want it anymore, and I certainly don't want the cleaning lady to find it tomorrow. That's the last thing I need getting out around here." He winked at me. "You can keep it as a souvenir." Then he walked out and gently shut the door behind him.

"Asshole," I muttered.

Chapter 17
Tyler

Punishing Victoria for her super-hot cock tease was one of the most satisfying things I'd ever done. And being inside of her? It was out of this world. It felt so good and so natural, it was no wonder that I'd almost lost control. I'd come so close to . . .

It was fucking scary.

I was losing my touch. My *edge*. And Victoria, with her body and dirty mouth, was to blame. I didn't want to believe it. I'd convinced myself I'd never have real feelings for a girl again. But if I went down the list of my feelings toward Victoria, it only further confirmed the truth of my addiction.

Can't stop thinking about her. Check.

Drives me crazy over the smallest things. Check.

Want to fuck her day and night. Check.

Do the stupidest shit around her. Check.

Yep, I was addicted alright. Addicted to the way she made me feel.

"There was no hot water," Victoria said, breaking me out of my reverie and appearing in the doorway of the bathroom connected to my room.

My heart thumped in my chest at the sight of her—her hair wet and wavy, her cheeks flushed with pink. She wore one of my black silk robes that was way oversized on her, but to me she looked like the hottest thing since sliced bread.

"You gotta' be shitting me," I said as I dug out some fresh boxers from my dresser and tossed them on my bed. I'd intended to jump in the shower right after. I was sticky down below after our session, but now I'd have to wait.

Or maybe I should take a cold shower to cool down my boiling blood, I thought.

"You would think things like that wouldn't happen in a place like this. That's ridiculous," she said, walking over to the dresser where her clothes were.

"It does that from time to time when they do maintenance," I explained. I picked up my boxers, preparing to go into the bathroom to get cleaned up. "In the meantime, take a load off. Stay for a bit."

"I'm not staying."

I froze, shocked. "Huh?"

Victoria grabbed her clothes and clutched them against her chest, hiding her stiff nipples. "I'm going home."

"Why the hell did you come all the way here if you were just going to go home?" I demanded. I hated how upset I sounded.

Victoria bit her lower lip. "I don't know. Maybe it was the way you ordered me to come, as if I didn't have a choice."

"Don't give me that." I growled. "You came because you wanted to."

"Either way, I'm leaving," Victoria said firmly. I could see the steel in her eyes. She was serious. I wasn't even sure if I could use my charm to get her to stay, but I wasn't about to beg. It pissed me off that I was even upset. Usually, I didn't even show them the door . . . that was Jonathan's job.

"Are you sure?" I hated even asking that much.

Victoria nodded and then tilted her head at the bathroom. "I'm going to go change into my clothes and then I'll be ready to go."

"I'll have Jonathan ready take you home."

On her way to the bathroom, Victoria paused to regard me. "You're not coming?"

"Nah. I think I'll take a shower and just relax."

She was a moment in replying. "Okay then."

While she went and changed, I told Jonathan to get the car ready to drop her off.

Victoria looked a rumpled mess when she appeared out of the bathroom, her skirt looking like it had a few holes in it from where I'd been rough. I made a mental note to buy her a new one.

"I hung your bath robe on the rack in there," she informed, doing her best to smooth her skirt.

"Alright," I said shortly. "Jonathan is waiting for you outside."

"Okay."

She walked over to the staircase leading down to the first floor of my loft. I hated myself for it, but I had to blurt, "Not even going to say bye?"

"Bye."

Then she was gone. I stood there for a long moment, varied emotions rolling through me, wondering why she'd suddenly decided she couldn't get away from me fast enough.

I know she enjoyed the sex, I thought. *What the fuck is going on?*

And that's what impressed me about Victoria. She made me work for it, something I'd never had to do before.

Victoria

I shouldn't have been so cold to him, I thought as Jonathan pulled the limo up closer. A pink corvette came swerving into the parking lot like a bat out of hell at the same time we were exiting, but I was too embroiled in my thoughts to notice.

It'd taken a lot to get the strength to leave, and I still wasn't exactly sure what it was that made me do so.

While I'd been taking a shower, all of my doubts and worries about Tyler's honesty came back to me and I suddenly found myself angry again. The strong emotion had made it easy for me to give him the cold shoulder and leave him with a bruised ego.

The image of the hurt in his eyes as I left flashed in my mind, making me feel a little sympathy, followed by a surge of anger.

Still, I had to admit the make-up sex in his office was off the charts. The whole thing had been exhilarating.

He only did it to show off his power over me. I bet he thought he

could just smooth everything over with his charm and I would just forgive
him because he fucked me good. Bastard.

I dug my fingers into my palm and angrily bit my lower lip, engaged in my thoughts. His cockiness pissed me off to no end. My skin burned as anger flared through my stomach . . . along with feelings of lust.

Fuck.

It pissed me off even more that even though I was mad at him, I still wanted him and couldn't stop fantasizing about him. I couldn't deny that the sex had been hot. Almost too hot. I didn't think I would ever experience something that sexy again. But did it matter if I did? In the end, I was just a fad, someone he could use against his dad to show his defiance. He still hadn't proven that I was anything to the contrary.

For most girls, the thought of being with Tyler Locklin would be a dream come true. For me, it was horrifying. That is, as long as I wasn't thinking about the sex.

I was the first girl who'd ever shown resistance to him, and he wanted to prove to himself that he could conquer me. And the whole thing with helping me start my own business? It upset me that I'd fallen for such an offer.

The limo rolling to a halt at a stop light brought me out of my thoughts. I reached for my purse to grab my cell, I needed to text April about an assignment at work . . . only to find it not there.

"God damn it," I muttered. "It took everything I had to leave. I won't be able to do that again. . ."

I mulled for a moment. We weren't that far away from the swanky apartment, but I wasn't sure I wanted to go back there. Showing back up after the cold front I gave Tyler would show that I was weak and needy.

But I need my phone.

Screw it, I thought finally. *I'll just run in, grab my purse and leave. I won't even look at him.*

"Jonathan," I called. "Can you go back to Tyler's apartment? I forgot something."

Tyler

I'd just gotten out of the shower, my hair wet, and dressed only in my boxers when I heard a noise that sounded like someone entering my apartment.

It's her.

I grinned, confident Victoria had changed her mind and decided to come back. My ego soaring, I stepped out of the bathroom, careful to keep my expression neutral and not too eager.

I couldn't keep the exultation out of my voice, though. "Back so soon—"

"Hey, Tyler!" chirped a familiar voice I hadn't heard in years.

My jaw dropped at the sight of the person standing at the doorway to my bedroom.

No. Fucking. Way. This bitch has balls.

I blinked, trying to will the image away.

Candice.

Am I hallucinating? I'm dreaming. I must be dreaming.

Candice, my old back-stabbing girlfriend, was standing there before me. Her hair was pulled back into a ponytail, short bangs framed her forehead, her makeup was soft and girly, and she was wearing a tight red dress that showed off her curvaceous figure that I once loved to handle.

I stood there, speechless, staring at her like she was a banshee that had come to haunt me.

It was she that had ruined my faith in relationships. Her, who I'd done everything for. Her, who I made sure wanted for nothing. I gave her everything.

All of me.

In the end, I found out she was just using me. Using me for my money and to get ahead. She had me fooled from the very beginning. I thought she was the love of my life, when all she ever was, was a fucking gold-digging skank.

"Still working out that incredible body, I see," she murmured with appreciation, eyeing my abs and appearing unperturbed by my shock.

Breath finally found my lungs. "What the hell are you doing here? And what makes you think you can waltz up in here like you own the place?"

Candice's eyes stayed on my abs. "You, or someone, left the door open," she replied softly, ignoring my question. "I knocked a few times. No one answered. I was going to leave, but I heard noises. I came in to check on you, to make sure you were alright. I called your name, but no one answered."

I cleared my throat, trying to regain my composure. "I was in the shower . . ."

Candice tore her eyes away from my stomach and nodded. "I realized that when I came up the stairs." She looked around the room. "Not much has changed, I see."

"Nope," I said easily, finally able to regain my swag. "But I have."

Candice stepped forward, reaching out. "Ty—"

"Don't even start!" I yelled.

Candice froze.

"Why are you here? You know how our relationship ended. I told you that I never wanted to speak to you or see you again. And I meant every word of it."

Candice's arms dropped to her side and she dipped her head. Seeing her look so vulnerable caused old emotions to roll through me. "I wanted to see you," she said quietly. "I've missed you."

"That boat has sailed," I said firmly, pushing away any feelings of sympathy. "Long ago. And it's not coming back."

Candice looked up. Tears were streaming down her face.

Oh God. Not this bullshit.

"I'm so sorry, Ty," she sobbed. "I didn't mean to do it. I've been trying to work up the courage for so long. It was just that I felt so lonely and so vulnerable and he—"

I set my jaw, unimpressed by her act. "Do you really think I want to listen to this bullshit? Good God, listen to

137

yourself! We will never be anything ever again, Candice. Ever!"

Candice pressed her hands against her face and sobbed, her whole body shuddering.

Damn, am I gonna have to drag her ass out of here or what? It was obvious that my ex-girlfriend wasn't going to make this easy for me.

"I'm not falling for it, Candice. You fooled me once with that shit, but you won't fool me again."

She stopped for a second. "It was the biggest mistake of my life! And I regret it more than anything in the world."

Ditto, I thought

"Can you quit with the act?" I demanded, after a half-second of listening to her ridiculous sobs. "It's pathetic."

Wiping her eyes, Candice grew quiet and stopped the melodramatic sobbing. It was crazy how she could cry her eyes out one minute and be totally tranquil the next. "I saw Jonathan help a girl inside of your limo as I was coming up. New girlfriend of yours?"

"That's none of your business."

"Really, Tyler? You could do so much better."

"Better than a cheating skank? I sure can."

Determined, Candice walked over to me, her intentional seductive strut seeming to taunt me. I averted my eyes, refusing to give her the satisfaction.

"What are you doing, Candice?" I growled, looking at the wall, even though I knew damn well what she was doing.

"It's been so long, Tyler," Candice purred, reaching me. She placed a hand against my stomach and then began dragging her fingers softly along my happy trail.

I grabbed her wrist firmly, stopping her before she could reach my junk. I turned my gaze on her, scowling fiercely. "I don't know why you suddenly decided to show up, Candice, or what you hope to accomplish, but I'm going to ask you one time to leave. If you don't, I'm going to drag your ass out of here. And trust me, you don't want me to do that."

Shit, I better be careful, I thought when something suddenly occurred to me. *Becoming forceful with her could be a lawsuit waiting to happen, maybe it's even exactly what she wants. She knows I'm loaded. If I get rough with her, she could claim anything, and being a female and with my bad boy reputation, who wouldn't believe her? I won't even have to worry about mine and Victoria's relationship ruining things at work. Candice will ruin everything herself.*

Worrying about whether Candice's intentions had malice in them caused me to become momentarily distracted and my grip on her wrist became lax, allowing her freedom.

"I bet whoever she is can't suck your dick like I can," Candice purred up at me, my cock suddenly in her grasp. "Remember? I'm the only one who could take all of you."

Before I could reply and shove the cock-hungry whore away, I heard a shocked gasp.

Chapter 18
Victoria

I'll just go up there, grab my purse, and leave. I'd repeated the litany about twenty times since getting out of the limo and making my way up to Tyler's door.

Don't show any emotion or give him a chance to get you in his bed.

All I had to do was keep telling myself that I was strong and that I could do it. The problem was, I could feel my resolve weakening.

There were too many conflicting emotions going through me.

On one hand, I wanted to believe Tyler. I wanted to believe he would be faithful with me and that we could somehow make our relationship work, even with our disapproving parents. If it wasn't for his past, I'd probably believe him. He hadn't given me much reason to doubt him, after all.

But, he *did* have his past. And our parents *did* want us apart. And I felt like he was just a rich, eligible bachelor who was looking for a challenge and a reason to defy his father.

After I exited the elevator at the top floor, I walked down the hallway. After a moment of gathering my resolve, I knocked on the door.

The door creaked open.

That's funny, I thought. *I thought I locked it.*

I stepped in and closed the door behind me. I was about to call out Tyler's name, when I heard talking up in the loft area where his bedroom was.

He must have company.

I walked over to the stairs and paused, listening. Then I heard it. A female's voice.

My heart began pounding in my chest erratically.

Calm down, I tried to tell myself. *It could be anyone.*

Despite trying to reason with myself and keep cool, I was overcome by a sudden, overpowering urge. I rushed up the stairs as fast as I could and let out a sharp gasp when I reached the top.

I knew it!

My wildly-beating heart skipped a beat at the sight before me.

There, standing before his bed with nothing on but boxers, was Tyler with some pretty blonde girl, dressed in a tight red dress, who was holding his cock in her hands.

You fool! How could you be so stupid?

The room began to spin around me and my breathing became shallow.

I should've known. I should've known. I should've known.

Tyler's expression was one of shock and he was quick to shove the girl away from him. "Victoria, I can explain!"

"Don't bother!" I croaked. I don't even know how I managed to get the words out. I had a lump in my throat the size of a basketball.

Fighting to keep the tears at bay, I rushed over to the night stand and grabbed my purse.

141

"Victoria!" Tyler reached out to grab my arm, but I swatted him away, rushing toward the exit.

"Don't fucking touch me!"

"Please—"

I stopped at the top of the stairs, digging in my purse, turning around to confront him.

"I knew from the beginning you were a sack of shit," I snarled. "I don't know how I could've been so stupid to ever believe that you actually cared about me or that you would stop your manwhore ways!"

Tyler reached out imploringly. "It's not what you think."

How cliché. Isn't that what they all say? It's not what you think. Everything I need to know is right in front of me.

In the background, the girl in the red dress watched our exchange with her hands on her hips and an impish smile on her face.

"He does this to all the girls, honey," she purred. "You shouldn't be surprised."

"Shut up, Candice!" Tyler shouted, his face red with rage. He turned to me. "Victoria—"

"Fuck off!" I reached into my purse to make sure my phone was there. I still had his tie . . . *that* tie. I pulled it out and threw it at his feet. "And you can keep your fucking nasty tie!"

Sobbing uncontrollably, I turned and rushed down the stairs, nearly tripping in the process.

Tyler

142

I stared at the spot Victoria had vacated long after she left, wanting to go after her but knowing it would be futile.

She'd walked in at the worst possible moment, just as Candice grabbed my junk. I'd never be able to convince her that nothing was going on.

Candice raised an eyebrow in question while eyeing the tie on the floor. "Do I even want to know what the deal with the tie is?" she asked, breaking the silence. "What kind of kinky shit have you been up to, Tyler?"

I turned baleful eyes on her, my chest heaving with anger. "Nothing that concerns you."

Bitch.

Rage blurred my vision. I wanted to wrap my hands around her neck and choke her within inches of her life. I'd never, ever put my hands on a woman in a violent way, but she was pushing me to my limits.

Looking at Candice, I could tell it's something that she probably wanted. She'd *love* it, in fact. In some sick way, she was feeding off my emotions, getting off on them.

"You need to leave," I said flatly. "Now. Or I'm going to call the cops."

I saw no use in trying to figure out why she was here or talking to her any further. It didn't matter anymore, and I should have thrown her out the second I saw her. But now, the damage was already done.

"Come on, Tyler," she crooned softly. "You're just mad right now. That girl . . . she was no good for you—"

"Get the fuck out!" I roared.

Candice grew silent in the face of my wrath. For a

143

moment, I feared she was going to stay, forcing me to have to take matters into my own hands.

"Fine," she said finally. "I'll leave . . . for now. I'll be back after I give you some time to calm down. You'll come around, you'll see. We have much to catch up on."

She walked over to me and attempted to give me peck on the cheek, but I stepped away from her. "I'm going to make things better. I promise." She turned and strutted her way out of the room, trying her best to tease me with her swaying hips.

She failed. "And don't fucking come back!" I yelled.

I walked over to the bed and slumped down on it, resting my elbows on my knees and clutching either side of my head in my palms.

"I'm fucked," I muttered.

Chapter 19
Victoria

"I hate to say it, but I told you so," April said the next day while we were preparing some of Christine's pristine spring designs for a show.

I groaned, eyeing a design, a particular ugly brown number that even a size one model would have to diet to fit in. "Please don't, April. I really don't need to hear this right now. On top of it all, I have a splitting headache."

I shouldn't have told her anything, I thought in regret. *Now I will never hear the end of it.*

As soon as I'd come into work, April accosted me. One look at my disheveled appearance, and she knew something was up. In fact, she knew *exactly* what was up.

Maybe it was my bloodshot eyes that were red from bawling my eyes out all night, or my perpetual scowl that I'd adopted when I woke up and realized I had to go to work when it felt like my soul was being crushed by an iron fist.

At first I'd deflected April's questions to find out what was wrong, but eventually I broke down and told her.

Everything.

I wasn't sure why I did. I mean, I knew what was coming afterward. I suppose it was because I needed a shoulder to cry on. Since I was estranged from my mom, April was the only real female friend that I was close enough to confide in.

I'd lost contact with all my previous friends when I moved to the city to start my career, and I couldn't just call them up to dump this in their lap after having not spoken for ages. Since coming to work for Christine, I'd discovered that friends were in short supply. It was hard maintaining friendships while being worked to death.

On top of that, I'd learned the hard way that there weren't many people you could trust in the fashion world, with all the back-stabbing and gossiping that went on.

But April, and to an extent, Gabe, were cool. So far, she hadn't shown me the cattiness that most females that worked under Christine were known for. She had her quirks, of course, but who didn't?

"What?" April protested. Today, April was dressed in a purple dress with a white belt encircling her waist. Matching white pumps adorned her feet. She looked cute, but then again, she always looked cute. Christine expected all of us to look great coming in to work. "But I was right, wasn't I? He was a manwhore all along. I mean come on, Vicky, how could you ever think he wasn't? The guy is filthy rich with movie star looks. Why would he want to settle down at his age? Besides, doesn't he normally go for the A-list starlets?"

I scowled at April. "I didn't think money or fame mattered when it came to love. Besides, he claimed to be attracted to me because of *me*, not my bank account, or lack thereof."

April shook her head, eying a flashy green number. "You're right. In some situations, money doesn't matter. As far as looks go, you could've looked like Kate Upton and he'd still have cheated on you. Guys like that just don't respect women. You should know that."

I bit my lower lip. Everything April was saying was true. I knew it, and she knew that I knew it. "You're right," I said grudgingly.

April stopped fingering the green number and slipped it onto a hanger before hanging it on one of the clothing racks lining the room. She turned to face me, crossing her arms. "Next time you should listen to me."

I snorted. "You're not Nostradamus, April. His past was no secret. But he seemed so sincere. So intense. But trust me, if I learned anything, it's that I'll always heed that annoying little voice inside my head from here on out."

April beamed at me. "Good. I'm just relieved that it happened now and not later. I certainly didn't want to see you more hurt than you already are."

A lump was forming in my throat. I wished she would just change the subject. "Gee, thanks, April."

"No problem. Trust me, you're so much better off without him."

"I think I'm done with relationships for now," I muttered.

And the distant future, I thought.

"Don't let him ruin your faith in men, though," April warned. "There are plenty of good ones out there. You just need to find the right one."

"For now, my career will be my man — or my pursuit of a career," I said, grabbing a red dress that had yellow flowers emblazoned on it. Now this was one I could see myself wearing.

"Fair enough—"

"Hey bitches!" chirped a cheery voice. Gabe came walking up and elbowed his way in between us. The always-handsome young man was dressed in skinny jeans and a preppy pink sweater, his hair gelled and slicked to the side. The smell of a fruity cologne wafted to my nose.

"Gabe," we both greeted in unison.

Gabe reared back when he looked at me, his face twisting in horror. "Sweet Jesus! What happened to you? You look like you were hit by a bus."

Before I could reply, April supplied, "Her big shot boyfriend cheated on her."

Gabe let out a gasp and clamped a hand over his mouth, his eyes going wide.

"April!" I protested.

"What? He would've found out anyway. You know he was going to hound you like hell to find out what was wrong."

"More like you would just tell him as soon as you saw him, like now," I accused.

April shrugged. "Same difference."

"Don't worry about me, Vicky," Gabe assured me, looking extra eager to hear the sensational gossip. "You know your business is safe with me, girl."

Right, I thought wryly. *You'll have my whole story all over the Channel Seven Evening News.*

"So tell me what happened," Gabe urged eagerly. "I want all the juicy details."

I groaned inwardly. *He's never going to give up. Thanks, April.*

I didn't want to keep rehashing the experience. It was

148

almost too painful. Luckily for me, or maybe not so lucky, April obliged me.

Gabe clamped a hand on my shoulder, shaking his head with sympathy when April was done with her slightly exaggerated tale of Tyler's cheating. "I am so sorry, girl. You must feel terrible. That man was sex on legs. Too bad he couldn't keep it in his pants."

"Can't we just change the subject already?" I demanded, tossing aside the red flower dress with exasperation. "I'm never going to get through the day if we don't."

Gabe frowned. "Okay. But can I ask a question?"

I sighed. "What?"

"How big is he?"

"Gabe!"

"What? We're talking about important information here!"

I scowled, wishing he'd just go away.

"Please, Gabe, I'm pretty sure he doesn't go for men. In fact, I know he doesn't."

Gabe raised a stern eyebrow at me. "I'll have you know, Miss Thing, that I've turned a few men in my day." Gabe crossed his arms. "But really, I do have a serious question."

I ignored him for as long as I could before I sighed and gave in. "What is it?"

"How is he in the sack?"

I tossed a dress right into Gabe's face, walking off and refusing to admit to him or anyone else that the sex was *amazing*.

Chapter 20
Charles

"I'm ready to take Tyler's place when you feel the time is right," I proudly announced to the CEO of Armex, hardly concealing my excitement. "Just say the word."

I'd stopped by Mr. James Locklin's office to have a talk about my soon-to-be promotion. Rumors were that Tyler's days were numbered and that I'd be his replacement. I hadn't been given the official word from Mr. Locklin about it yet, but I had to come across as confident and willing to do the job.

Pride swelled through me as James, who was sitting at a large desk in the center of room, leaned back in his chair to regard me.

"Ah, Mr. Whitmore. As one of my best employees, I've always admired your enthusiasm for this company and your willingness to do what's best for our bottom line."

A feeling of dread pressed down upon my chest. The tone in his voice told me something was afoot. There was a *BUT* coming . . .

I smiled nervously and nodded my head. "Thank you, sir. It's my pleasure. Working for Armex has been a dream come true for me."

I was laying it on pretty thick, hoping that my feeling was wrong. James shifted in his seat, and by his expression, I knew he was about to hit me with something. "That being said, I have no intention of removing my son as CFO."

Well fuck me gently with a chainsaw . . .

It felt like I'd been hit by a bolt of lightning. "What?" I asked in disbelief. I'd all but been assured by everyone else that Tyler's position was mine. "I was told that this was a done deal!"

"I'm sorry, Charles, but this whole thing got started because I reacted out of anger."

I couldn't believe what I was hearing. I was usually a composed individual, but it was hard to keep a lid on my frustration. My dreams and aspirations were crashing down around me. "You said yourself that I understood the intricacies of running this company better than anyone you'd ever met!"

James scowled. "No, what I in fact told you, was that you take your job very seriously, and I appreciated that. But Tyler is my son, and as much as I want him to get his life together, I can't aid in taking this from him. My conscience just won't allow it. I'm willing to accept whatever consequences come from it."

You've got to be shitting me.

I clenched my fists, anger swelling in my throat. "I can't believe you're saying this, sir," I said hotly. "You're going to let Tyler continue to be the downfall of Armex? *Your* company?"

James sat silent.

"Why?" I continued. "Why would you want to keep someone like that on board, even if he is your son, when you have someone more capable and far more willing to take this company to the next level?" I shook my head. "I just don't get it."

"You are both alike," James remarked, his eyes scrutinizing me.

"Never!" I raged. "I'm nothing like him."

"Yet, in some ways you are. You're so blinded by your dislike and jealousy of my son that you fail to see it. In my opinion, you both are hard-headed and have a problem with authority."

I sucked in a breath, readying a hot retort, but then gained control of myself. "Are you alright, sir? You sure you haven't drunk anything, taken any medication?" It was unlike James to be so direct with me. Maybe he was speaking under the influence.

"I'm perfectly sober."

"I—"

James stood up from his chair, interrupting me, looking tall and imposing. I could definitely see where Tyler got his impressive frame from. James was the type of old man you didn't want to mess with you. "I want what's best for my son, Charles. He's my only heir. This company is just as much his as it is mine. I have to believe that he'll turn things around, however unlikely that may be."

"But you're making a business decision based on emotion, sir," I protested. "That's like the number one no-no in business. You know that even more than I do."

"Even so, you have my decision. I can only hope Tyler straightens up and becomes the man that I know him to be." He looked at me with sympathy. "I'm sorry, Charles. I know you were looking forward to this."

"Weak," I snarled. I knew I was insulting my boss, a very powerful man, but I couldn't help myself, and my emotions were getting the better of me. "This decision makes you look weak and unfit."

"I know very well how it makes me look," James said tightly, "and if you value your place here at Armex, I suggest you watch what you say right now. I know you're upset and speaking out of emotion right now, so I'll forgive you this once, but make no mistake, I will not tolerate any more disrespect." His eyes bore into me. "Do I make myself clear?"

I stood there for a long time, overwhelmed by helpless rage.

"Charles?"

"Yes," I grated. "Yes sir, I understand you completely."

James nodded his head. "Good. Now go finish that report that you said you would have on my desk by Monday." He sat down at his desk and began looking over a stack of papers, letting me know our meeting was over.

Swallowing my pride, I turned and walked out of the office, closing his door a little louder than I should have behind me, vowing that it was time to take matters into my own hands. This wasn't over, not by a long shot.

Chapter 21
Tyler - Three Months Later

An irritating beeping sound awoke me with a start. I laid there for a while, trying to ignore it before I went searching for the annoying offender.

"Shut the fuck up," I growled. The sounds literally felt like they were skull-fucking me, sending sharp slashes of pain through my temples.

Rolling over in bed, moaning and groaning, I blindly ran my fingers over my night stand until I hit the alarm clock button, narrowly missing knocking over a half empty bottle of vodka.

"Fuck, my head hurts," I groaned, clutching at my temples.

I felt like complete shit, but that was to be expected.

I'd spent another night out, drinking and partying at the hottest clubs the city's night life had to offer, attempting to drown away my unhappiness. I hadn't been in this much of a slump since Candice . . .

Speaking of Candice, since leaving my apartment the night she unceremoniously showed up, Victoria had refused to return any of my calls.

For three months straight.

I'd left her more messages than I could count, messages that I'd be ashamed of under ordinary circumstances. Messages where I'd poured my heart out and tried to explain my situation and what actually happened.

It didn't work. She was as stubborn as me sometimes, and maybe that's why I liked her so much.

I'd even tried to track her down at work, but I never seemed to be able to catch her. She either wasn't there or someone would tell me she was too busy running errands for Christine. I figured it was probably bullshit, but I wasn't going to push it and get her in trouble, making everything worse.

Her coworker, April, appeared to take a special glee in turning me away. She always had this huge smile on her face, pissing me off even more. She knew it too. I could tell.

Finally, I'd given up on making myself look pathetic. I got very angry at Victoria, even told myself that I didn't need her. That I was better than her. After all, I was a rich CFO with my whole life ahead of me, standing to be the sole beneficiary to an empire. There wasn't a girl on the planet that wouldn't want to be with me.

Except *one*. The one I wanted.

She needed *me*. I didn't need her, I told myself. She'd regret her decision for the rest of her life. I just knew it.

Distraught, I turned to alcohol to numb the pain of our break up. I felt weak for doing it, but I could find no other respite.

Sure, I could've gone out and had revenge sex with every willing slut that I could find. After all, isn't that what Victoria thought of me? A manwhore who couldn't keep his big dick in his pants?

Maybe I was once that man, but strangely enough, those things no longer interested me. I wanted one thing and one thing only.

Victoria.

My phone beeped, drawing me out of my reverie.

Wiping the sleep out of my eyes, I grabbed it off the night stand, this time knocking over the bottle of Vodka.

I'll just have Jonathan clean it up, I thought as the smell of alcohol hit my nostrils.

It took several seconds for my fuzzy mind to read the reminder I'd set on my phone.

ARMEX meeting today.

"Shit," I muttered.

* * *

"You looked like shit today in the meeting," Jeff hissed. "What is wrong with you?"

Me and my fellow colleague were sitting in my office after a nearly disastrous meeting where I'd been unable to read my report without stumbling over my words. It'd gotten so bad that my dad had to step in to save me from further embarrassing myself.

He hadn't looked too happy about that. In fact, he looked like he wanted to choke me with his bare hands. I knew that we were going to have words later, and I wasn't looking forward to it.

I was barely holding it together as it was.

I lowered my head to my desk and groaned. "Don't you have something better to do? I don't want to hear this shit."

"Well, you're going to hear it, because I've never seen you act so disgusting inside that room before. And the only reason why you're still sitting in that chair and not out looking for a job is because of your father."

I looked up, then winced a second later as my temples pounded. The four Tylenol I'd taken before the meeting had done little to alleviate my misery. "That's not true," I croaked. "I'm here because I'm valuable."

Jeff snorted. "Listen to yourself, Tyler! Get a grip and come back to planet Earth. It's time to stop disrespecting your father and this company!"

Anger surged through me. "Who the fuck are you to judge me, huh?" I snarled, immediately regretting it as a sharp pain sliced through my skull. Seriously, it felt like someone took an axe and brought it down on the top of my head with all the force they could muster. "You have no fucking idea what I'm going through."

Jeff let out a peal of derisive laughter. "Oh, poor little baby and his first world problems. Did the latest slut decline letting you bang her brains out and your little ego is bruised?"

Seriously, the only thing keeping Jeff from being thrown through my window and falling sixty stories was the lancing pain in my skull.

"Get over it," Jeff continued, unaware how lucky he was to be alive. He stood, straightening his tie at his neck. "You're a disgrace."

He turned and walked out of my office, slamming the door behind him. The sound of it made my head hurt even worse.

Asshole.

Despite my anger at Jeff, deep down I knew he was speaking the truth. I had to get my shit together.

Fast.

Chapter 22
Tyler

"Victoria is busy," April said to me. She gave me that *ha-ha asshole, you'll never talk to her again* smirk. "But I can give her a message if you'd like?"

After a couple of days of torment, I'd stopped the drinking, cleaned myself up, and decided on a new course of action.

I'd driven myself—something I almost never do—over to Victoria's workplace. When I asked the receptionist on the first floor to ring me in to Victoria's work phone, April had appeared instead to take a message.

I swear the girl had become Victoria's bodyguard, appearing out of the woodwork whenever I showed up, intent on making sure that I didn't get anywhere near her.

I eyed her with a cool grin on my face, not letting her think she was getting to me. Not even that long ago, I'd have been eager to wipe that smirk off of the little tart's face . . . and I'm not talking about with my hand or with violence.

"She needs to hear something directly from me, not from a message. If she doesn't want to speak to me again after that, I'll never bother her again."

April stared at me suspiciously and I adopted my most serious expression. "Really. She's going to want to hear this, trust me."

April stood there for the longest time, looking like a battle was going on inside of her head. Finally, she let out a huge sigh. "I'll go find her and see what she says." She turned away, but stopped to add, "On one condition."

"Anything."

"You never come here again."

If I get to talk to her, I won't need to come here again, I thought.

"Scout's honor," I assured, putting up the little hand signal.

April scowled at me, looking as if she was going to change her mind. I kept my expression straight and serious.

"Okay," she finally said. "Don't make me regret this or you'll be sorry."

"I won't," I promised.

She still looked skeptical. "Wait here and I'll be right back."

I spent the better of twenty minutes standing around at the receptionist's desk, looking like a dumbass waiting for April to come back. The receptionist, Kathy, a middle-aged woman with graying hair, kept me entertained, telling me all about her daughter and her recent engagement. She seemed to be that type of person who'd talk to just about anyone and tell them her life story.

"She's so happy," Kathy was saying to me after just showing me her daughter, a little blonde with a humble next-door type appearance. "She got herself a good fella—handsome too, just like yourself." She beamed at me.

"Oh you're so kind," I said, trying to sound at least a little interested in the conversation. "Truth be told, there's nothing special about my looks."

"Handsome and modest, a good combination," Kathy said, placing the back of her hand to the side of her mouth and lowering her voice to a conspirator whisper, "You'd be quite the catch."

"Modest, huh?" I chuckled. "Now that's something I haven't heard before."

At that moment, April reappeared, walking up the hallway toward me. The look on her face told me everything.

"Sorry, I have to go," I said, not sparing Kathy another glance. "It was nice meeting you, Kathy." I walked off briskly before the she could reply, making it to April in several quick strides.

"Well?" I demanded, trying to keep myself calm and collected.

April stared at me for what seemed like an eternity, purposefully drawing the moment out.

Finally, she said, "Against my better judgment, Victoria's willing to talk to you."

* * *

I tapped my fingers impatiently against the wooden armrest of my chair. This was so not me, being forced to wait to be seen. Usually it was the other way around. April had led me to a waiting room on the top floor of the building. It had a pretty nice view, but nothing like what I enjoyed at my office.

The problem was that, while nice and all, Christine's building wasn't high enough to see over all the other surrounding buildings, so all you saw were other buildings blocking out the view.

I turned my eyes away from the outside, my thoughts going inward. I wondered what had been going on with Victoria all this time. Had she thought about me? Would she forgive me? I didn't know the answers to these questions, but that's what I intended to find out.

I was going to do my best to win her back. I already knew how I was going to prove to her that what she saw with Candice wasn't what it looked like.

All I needed was the chance . . . and I could set things right.

After what seemed like an eternity, the door cracked open and I quickly sprang to my feet like a jack-in-the-box. My heart began to pound in my chest in an annoying fashion as I waited for the door to open fully. I waited, holding my breath, preparing myself for what I had to say.

Don't screw this up, Ty.

The door open and in walked . . . *What the fuck?*

Christine Finnerman.

She was dressed like the frigid ice queen that she was, in a form-fitting white dress with a matching white belt at her waist, frosted pumps, her silver hair done up into an elegant style. A sparkling necklace adorned her neck, which was tight and firm for a woman of her age.

Though I'd never met Victoria's boss, I knew how she looked because of the billboards that had her evil mug plastered on them all over city.

All in all, I'd say she was one of the state's most powerful women. Her name commanded respect.

"What's going on here?" I asked in confusion as Christine

slowly closed the door behind her. I looked over her shoulder, somehow hoping Victoria had followed in behind her. "Where's Victoria?"

Christine's gaze centered on me like a hawk, her eyes blazing with hatred.

I'm usually a guy that can't be ruffled, but this woman made me hot under the collar . . . and not in a good way. I swore if she kept looking at me like that, I'd catch on fire.

"She's not coming," she said crisply, her voice as cold and frigid as she looked. "You'd do well to forget all about her."

I stood my ground. "What do you mean she's not coming? She's a grown woman and can make her own decisions. You're not her mother. Is this another one of your attempts to make her life a living hell?"

"I'm just her employer, something you forgot when you filled her little head with that startup nonsense." She grinned tightly. "Fortunately for her, I saw right through what was happening and chose to give her mercy by keeping her employed here."

"Please," I scoffed. "Being tortured working under you is what you call mercy? Give me a break!"

I expected a hot retort. Instead, Christine began to circle me. "In a way, I'm the only mother she's got."

I laughed in disbelief. "You're unbelievable. And I thought I was full of myself."

Christine looked at me as if waiting for me to say something else. When I didn't, she spoke up.

"You know, when I saw Victoria standing in front of me that first day, interviewing for a position as one of my assistants,

163

I saw a girl who was vulnerable, lost. I saw a girl who needed guidance. I thought, *she reminds me of me when I was younger.* I took her under my wing, Mr. Locklin, because I had a gut feeling that Victoria had a future ahead of her, a career that will never be allowed to flourish with you underfoot."

"Nice story," I said sarcastically, "but what a load of bullshit! Victoria has told everyone who will listen about how horrible and awful you treat her. And now you want to act like you're her fairy godmother?!"

"Ah, yes," Christine said, "big, bad, evil Christine, treating her girls like they're red-headed stepchildren." She clasped a hand to her cheek. "Whatever shall they do?" She circled me again, stopping directly in front of me. This time, her gaze softened as she looked me in the eyes. "We live in a cruel world, Mr. Locklin, as I'm sure you know, working in the corporate world and all, and there is nothing crueler than to work in the cut-throat world of fashion. What these girls think is mean, is actually me preparing them for the viciousness that awaits them. I do it and I make no apologies about it either, because if Victoria doesn't crack under the pressure, she'll appreciate it later. If she does, then this business just wasn't for her."

"That was a nice little speech," I growled, doing a quick golf clap that was meant to annoy her. "You almost convinced me with that one. Now let me see Victoria."

Christine's face hardened into stone. "Victoria is busy, Mr. Locklin. Besides, you'd be better off focusing on helping your father's company maintain its portfolio rather than wasting your time on Victoria. Now please, I'm going to need you to leave my building."

Ignoring the last bit, I said "You're not accomplishing anything. You can't keep me from seeing her."

Christine produced a cellphone out of the side of her dress in one quick, elegant flourish, brandishing it in front of my face as if it were a weapon. "Of course I can't. But I can have you escorted out of the building. Which I'll be forced to do if you don't leave within ten seconds." She stared at me with challenge. I could see in her eyes that she wanted me to defy her.

I stood there for a second, wondering if I should call her bluff.

"Fine," I said, hating myself for giving up, but not wanting to give the condescending woman the pleasure of having me removed from her building. "I'm leaving."

Victoria

I let out a sigh, sweat beading my forehead. When I'd gotten the message from April that Tyler was here, I almost lost my will, tempted to go down to talk to him. Right when I was about to go down, Christine intervened, saying that she'd handle it and if I wanted to see him, I'd have to do it on my own time.

While there was the normal *bossiness* in her voice, it almost sounded like she said it as *I got your back*. I was shocked, but at the same time, I was probably just imagining it. Christine never did anything for anyone, though she had seemed to lighten up a little over the last couple of months.

"What did he say?" I asked with trepidation, not sure if I

wanted to know the answer.

Ignoring him was the hardest thing I'd ever done, but I'd managed. All I had to do was think of what I'd seen, and it gave me the will and the resolve to hold steady.

Today was the first time that the image didn't produce the strength needed to resist the urge to give him a chance to explain.

"He was determined to see you," Christine replied. "I told him that you were busy, which you are. Victoria, I don't need this kind of thing happening here. I know you can't control him, but I need you to try to ensure this doesn't happen again."

I was taken back, almost speechless. "Um, thank you, Mrs. Finnerman," I told her, unsure exactly what to say. "And it won't happen again. I promise."

Christine walked over. "Good. Now get back to work. You're a good assistant with a bright future ahead of you, but trust me with this one: there's a thousand girls out there who'd kill for your job, and I won't tolerate disruptions."

My jaw almost needed to be picked up from my desk. Did Christine just compliment me? What was the world coming to?

"Close your mouth, Victoria, or you might catch a fly," Christine advised, knowing that she'd just rendered me speechless.

I snapped my mouth shut as my boss walked away. "And don't let my praise go to that silly little head of yours, Victoria. You have a long way to go before you can walk a step in my shoes."

And then she was gone.

Chapter 23
Tyler

"You don't have to worry about me embarrassing you anymore," I said to my father as I sat directly across from him in his office. "My relationship with Victoria is over."

My father regarded me wearily. "Is that why you suddenly started drinking?"

I nodded. Normally I didn't reveal private things that involved emotion with him, but I felt like I needed to, so that we'd be able to at least function on speaking terms for the betterment of Armex.

"Yes. We haven't seen each other for a few months now, actually."

"I suppose that explains a lot," Dad muttered. He stared at me. "I'm sorry, son. How are you doing?"

I shrugged. "I'm over it."

"Don't try to act all nonchalant with me, Tyler." Dad sat back in his seat. "For a while I didn't believe you cared about Victoria one way or the other. I believed you were just using her to get back at me because I wanted you to have a perfect relationship. In reality, I should have been happy you finally found someone who could rein you in. Lord knows you've picked some real keepers. Like . . ."

"Don't even mention her name," I growled.

He cleared his throat. "Anyway, after I thought about it, I

realized standing in your way was just going to make matters worse."

Gee, Dad, I thought wryly. ***Now*** *you want to come to this conclusion when our relationship is over. How convenient.*

I saw no use in arguing about it. What was done, was done.

I held in a groan. I really didn't want to hear all this now after all I'd gone through. After all, what good did it do me? I was dead to Victoria.

"All of that doesn't matter anymore," I said flatly. "It's over, so you can stop worrying about me ruining the company's image, making a fool of myself or going around screwing anything that moves. I'm done with all that. For good."

"That's music to my ears. But I just want you to be happy, son," Dad said empathically. "That's all I've ever wanted from the beginning."

I snorted. "You sure have a hell of a way of showing it. You threatened to replace me with Charles Whitmore. I mean, I would've been pissed either way, but Charles Whitmore? I can't stand that guy and you know it!" I'd intended to keep my cool during our little talk, but I was shocked at the anger that came through my voice.

Dad made a 'calm down' motion with his hand. "Relax, Ty. I never had any intention of replacing you with Charles. Well, maybe for a minute out of anger. Of course I knew you were rivals. I hoped that telling you he would take your spot would light a fire under your ass."

"Well how'd that work out?" I muttered sourly.

Dad ignored me. "And there's another thing, Ty." He

paused and I knew whatever he was about to say was difficult for him. "I'm sorry . . . for pressuring you to break up with Victoria. Sometimes, I feel like we're more alike than you know. When someone tells us not to do something, it makes us want to do it that much more."

I grew silent. For my dad to apologize . . . well, it was unheard of. I can't remember him ever saying those words to me before for *anything*. He wasn't as prideful as me, but he was damn near close.

"Um, thanks, Dad," I said awkwardly. "I know that must've been tough."

Dad wiped at sweat that was suddenly beading his forehead. "You can say that again."

I stood up out of my chair and stretched out my arms, suddenly eager to get away. "Alright, I'm going to go. Got a report I need to finish. See you tomorrow." I turned to leave.

"Wait."

I paused. "Huh?

"One last thing." He fiddled with one of his favorite pens, a gift I'd gotten him one Christmas that was emblazoned with gold and personalized with his name. "If you should somehow get back with Victoria . . . you have my blessing."

Chapter 24
Tyler

"Shit, I feel like the world is crashing down on my head," Brad groaned, downing a shot. He let out a heavy sigh and smacked the glass back down on the bar, rattling my glass of Sprite. "The wedding is two weeks from now."

Brad had called me to meet up with him to discuss his upcoming wedding and the anxiety he had over it. Not having anything particularly important happening, I was quick to oblige. I seem to have a lot more free time on my hands these days.

"Everything is going to work out fine," I assured him. "I got everything covered. Stop worrying, stop stressing. It's not worth it."

Brad regarded me with bloodshot eyes. "Well, just look at Positive Suzy over here. Everything is just flowers and rainbows for you, isn't it?"

I fingered my cold glass of Sprite, wishing it was something stronger. "You called me here to give you support. I'm giving it, but if you want, I can tell you how stupid you are and how your life is over instead."

Brad shook his head. "Nah, nah. You're right. I should stop being such a little bitch. It's just that . . ." He groaned. "Katie won't stop talking about babies! I mean, what's wrong with her? I'm just getting going with my career, and she literally wants to conceive on our honeymoon." Brad signaled the

171

waitress to bring him another glass and promptly turned it up as soon as it arrived. "Fuck, man."

Babies. Just even thinking about the concept felt alien to me. I'd never really given much thought to the idea, never really wanted a kid except for maybe when my youth was gone and I was too old to do all the things I loved to do.

For some reason, the thought of babies brought Victoria to my mind. Her pretty smile. Her stubborn personality. I could totally see us having . . .

In panic, I pushed the troublesome thoughts away. *I must be getting old*, I thought.

"You need to put your foot down," I told him. "Now instead of later. Have a talk before the wedding. Come to an understanding."

"Ugh," Brad groaned. "I don't know."

I placed a hand on Brad's shoulder. "Look, a healthy relationship is based on equal partnership, not a dictatorship. A considerate and loving partner will listen to your wants and needs and take them into consideration when they come into conflict with their own. You should be able to tell Katie yours, and then you guys should be able to discuss things and find a happy medium. I mean, come on. If you guys can't see eye to eye now, how do you expect to remain married? Why get married in the first place?"

Look at me sounding like I'm some sort of therapist, I thought. For some reason, being without Victoria had made me become all preachy.

Brad stared at me for an entire minute before he spoke. I wondered if he could even comprehend what I was saying.

172

"Who the fuck are you? I mean, you look like Tyler. At least I think you do. I'm pretty drunk, after all. But you know what?" he asked. "Whoever you are, you're right. I should have a talk with her, let her know who's boss."

"There you go," I said. "Grow some balls."

Brad snorted. "I've always had balls. Katie's just had a grip on them for the longest time. A sharp, nail-filled grip."

I winced at the image his words summoned.

"But now she's talking about buying a house as soon as we're back from the honeymoon—you know—a place to put said babies in," he moaned, looking like he was about to fall apart.

I tightened my grip on his shoulder. "Remember what I said," I reasoned. "Talk it out like two adults. Everything will be fine."

Or run now while you still can, I thought. *Run far, far, away. Save your sanity.*

I didn't bother saying what I was thinking. I knew that Brad was dead set on marrying her, despite all of his complaining. He loved Katie more than life itself.

"I hope so."

"Trust me, it will."

I'll be surprised if he even attempts to talk to her, I thought. *And if he does, the conversation probably won't last but a minute before he just caves into whatever she wants.*

"Enough of me; have you heard anything from Victoria?" Brad asked.

A sharp pain stabbed through my chest. "We haven't seen each other for a while now."

173

"I'm sorry, man," Brad slurred. "She was a pretty girl. *Pretty wasn't the start of it.*

"It's alright," I lied. "I've had worse happen to me."

Our conversation drifted to more mundane matters, Brad talking about his law firm and the raise he was looking forward to, while I talked about how much better Armex was doing now that I had my shit together.

"You're still on to be my best man, right?" Brad slurred as his head seemed to be bouncing around like a bobblehead.

To be honest, I really didn't want to go to the wedding. I was just getting over my depression, and a cheery celebration would only make it worse. I felt like it would remind me of what I lost . . .

"You *are* coming, right?" Brad persisted. "After you spent all that money on those high-fashioned outfits, it would be a shame if you didn't."

A jolt of lightning went through me.

Fashion! That's it!

"Fuck, Brad," I said, clapping him hard on the back. "You're a genius."

Brad peered at me stupidly. "Tell me something I don't know, will ya?"

I gulped down my entire glass of Sprite and grinned. "Never mind."

"Shit. You're acting more hammered than I am and you haven't taken one sip."

"Must be the those flowers you were talking about earlier."

Brad groaned, grabbing at his temples. "Whatever, man.

174

My fucking head hurts. I know I'm going to wake up to a disgusting hangover tomorrow." He paused to stare at me. "You are coming to the wedding, though, right?"

Adopting an assuring smile, I draped an arm over Brad and signaled the waitress. Maybe I'd have a drink after all.

"I'll be there, buddy."

Chapter 25
Victoria

"I'm sorry, Christine isn't available right now, can I take a message?" I asked.

"No, you can't," said the frigid woman's voice on the other end of the line. "Just tell her that I, or my models, won't be attending since she doesn't have the decency to be available when I need her most."

Click.

What the hell was that about?

Setting down the phone, I let out a frustrated sigh, blowing my bangs out of my eyes. I was having a stressful day. Christine had chosen to take the day off for some unknown reason, leaving me to take a million messages. I'd taken up residence in her office, and I would've been flattered by sitting in her seat if not for all the stress that came along with it.

Now she's going to blame me for Mrs. White canceling, I thought. *Even though I have no idea why.*

Patty White was a popular fashion designer that was supposed to be Christine's friend, and she usually supported all of Christine's events.

Apparently something must've happened between the two. Whatever it was, it must have been pretty bad for her to pull something like that. Christine's summer events were all the talk in the business.

"Just great," I muttered as I fingered through Christine's event planner, found Patty's name, and put a note to the side. "Just one more thing for her to bitch about when she comes back."

A knock at the doorway caused me to jump.

"Hey new boss lady!" April chirped cheerfully, popping her head through the doorway. "When did the wicked witch die and make you the new queen?" She stepped fully into the room, a stack of papers in her hands.

As usual, I thought she looked adorable. Her hair was pulled into two little girl ponytails on either side of her head, and she wore a white tank top and a white skirt embroidered with some kind of sparkly studs. Spiked boots adorned her feet.

If there was one thing I could say about April—she knew how to dress.

I groaned. "Please don't. I'm already nauseous and the day isn't half over yet."

"Oh please, I would kill to be in that chair," said April.

I stood up and motioned to Christine's seat, which we all had dubbed 'The Throne'. "Be my guest."

April clutched her papers to her chest and shook her head, her tails shaking about. "Nope. She put you in charge, not me. Though why she did that boggles my mind."

Actually, Christine had eased up quite a bit since Tyler had shown up. She hadn't been Mother Theresa by any standards—she was Christine Finnerman, after all. But she'd started to give me a little more responsibility, like today, for example. All of the useless errands she used to put me on, she made the newer girls do. I appreciated it and welcomed the experience.

"I'm basically here to take messages, not much else. But I agree, she has been a little different."

"Must be something in the water," April muttered. Then she shook her head. "But you might want to sit back down, because you might not like what I'm about to tell you."

"What?" I demanded, gripping the edge of Christine's desk, my heart beginning to pound. I eyed the papers April held with a sneaking suspicion.

"Christine was supposed to be a panelist for a modeling audition today."

"Huh?" I asked in confusion. I was relieved and confused at the same time, and I had no idea what April was talking about. I usually handled Christine's schedule, and I knew nothing about this.

"The male modeling auditions for Christine's underwear line. It's today. From time to time, Christine sits in. I thought you knew that?"

Before I could reply, April continued talking. "Anyway, me, Gabe and a couple of our co-workers are sitting in." She beamed at me, shaking her pony tails with glee. "And guess who is filling in for Christine?"

"Me?" I squeaked in disbelief.

April nodded, jumping up and down with excitement.

"But she didn't even tell me this!" I protested. I'm all for the extra responsibility, but I didn't know the first thing about judging models, especially male models. Not only that, Christine hadn't told me a thing about it, robbing me of the chance to prepare.

If I held them to the standards to Tyler, they'd probably all come up short anyway.

I had no idea why I thought of that right then.

"It's Christine. I don't question anything she does," April said. "I learned that a long time ago."

"Oh God," I groaned. This is going to be a nightmare.

"Don't worry," April soothed. "Look at the bright side, at least you get to look at some hot guys modeling underwear. There's going to be so much eye candy you'll get sick! Heck, maybe you can even find you a cute guy to have some fun with."

"Please," I muttered, rolling my eyes.

April laughed and glanced down at her watch. "Come, let's go. The models are going to start pouring in here in the next fifteen minutes. We need to have our butts glued to our chairs ten minutes before."

"Alright, alright!" I conceded, grabbing one of Christine's notebooks off her desk. "I'm coming."

* * *

By the time we got to the auditioning room, I was at least somewhat versed on how to judge the models.

Of course I can pick who I think has the best body, but I was told to give preference to those that were in a particular age bracket and had an *edgy* look. They had to be fit, but not overly muscular.

The auditioning room was large, with brick walls and clothing racks lining the perimeters. A table, where the judges were sitting, was at the back of the room, and a large platform where the models would be standing was erected in front of it.

April and I made our way to the table. I quickly greeted

Gabe and my co-workers and then sat down beside April in the middle seat. After a moment of discussion, the auditions began.

"Bring them on in," April called, clapping her hands together.

"Oh, I so can't wait for this," Gabe said excitedly, wiggling in his seat.

Oh god, I thought. Gabe was going to have a fucking field day with this.

On April's command, one of the waiting interns opened the doors and a line of men wearing just white underwear flowed into the room.

Though I'd seen men in their underwear before, I couldn't keep from blushing at all the bared flesh before me. And bulges. So. Many. Bulges.

Just keep repeating to yourself they're all gay, I told myself. *So you don't get any ideas to procreate.*

It was hard, though, with so much temptation in front of me. This type of job definitely was *not* for me. And if I was having trouble focusing, Gabe definitely shouldn't be here.

Chiseled jaws, chiseled thighs, chiseled abs everywhere. Perfect, white smiles. Almost too perfect.

April smiled at the first round of men that lined the platform. "Thank you all for coming. The wonderful Mrs. Christine Finnerman couldn't be here today, so her right hand assistant, Victoria, will be sitting in her place helping us judge. You all will be judged by certain criteria that Christine is looking for right now. If you're a good fit, you'll be called back in. If you don't hear back from us . . . well, you can always try again next time. Christine is always changing what she's looking for, so don't get discouraged if you're not chosen." April looked around at all the young, half-naked men. "Any questions?"

Most of the them shook their heads.

April smiled wider. "Alright, let's begin. First man up! Please state your name before walking down the runway."

"Aubrey."

Aubrey was a skinny blonde guy, with high cheekbones, blue eyes, and an average package . . . though we weren't supposed to be judging bulge sizes. Besides that, he certainly fit the bill, but I wasn't too impressed by him.

Aubrey walked down the platform onto the runway with an awkward gait, his expression stoic and lifeless. He posed for a moment and then walked toward the judges, turned, and then made his way back onto the platform.

April scribbled something on her notebook and I wondered if I should be doing the same.

"He's too skinny," Gabe whispered. "Even by industry standards."

"Well?" April pressed me. "We don't have all day, Vicky. You gotta be quick."

"I wasn't impressed," I admitted finally, feeling sick to my stomach.

April nodded and then turned to beam happily at the young man. "Thank you for coming, Aubrey. You'll hear back from us if you're selected." I watched her cross the young man's name off the list as he walked off.

"Don't worry about it, honey," Gabe whispered to me, seeing the trepidation on my face. "That guy will find work with one designer or the other. And stop worrying about judging

181

these dudes. They got into modeling to be judged on their looks and bodies, and if they can't handle it, they don't need to be in this business."

Gabe's words did little to ease me of my anxiety as the next guy stepped up.

"Jake."

Jake was tall and auburn-haired with a masculine jawline and a toned body. I had to admit that I liked what I saw.

He walked down the walkway with a smile, winking at the judge table before walking back. Even his butt was cute.

"He's a keeper," Gabe whispered immediately.

In thought, April chewed her pen for a second and turned to me. "What do you think?"

"I'm with Gabe, but are we supposed to sit here and discuss them all or can we just scribble down our thoughts and move this along?"

April stared at me for a moment before shaking her head. "Just trying to get you used to it all, honey." She turned her head to Jake. "Thank you, Jake." She smiled at the handsome man. "Next!"

I sat through the next wave of models, trying to be the best judge I could be. I hated every time I had to be truthful and vote against a candidate, but over time my anxiety waned just a bit. I realized that I had a long way to go before I could even aspire to be in a position similar to Christine.

An hour later, and we'd dwindled the room down to just a dozen or so remaining. The eye candy was nice and all, but I'd had enough. I was ready to go.

After another contestant left, I took a sip of the bottled

water I had in front of me and lowered my head to check my notes while the next guy stepped up and announced his name.

"Tyler."

My head snapped up fast at the deep, familiar baritone. I *knew* that voice. But it can't be, can it?

What in the hell?

There, standing on the platform like he owned it and making the other men around him look like little boys, was Tyler in all of his masculine glory, a cocky grin on his face and that mischievous sparkle in his eyes.

How the hell did I miss him?

I froze, staring at Tyler, who was looking at me with that grin that I'd found so hard to resist. My whole body was trembling.

April seemed to still have her wits about her. "What are you doing here, Mr. Locklin?" she demanded.

Tyler kept his eyes on me. "What do you mean? I'm here to model underwear . . . like everyone else."

April scowled. "Really? All you're doing is disrespecting the judges and all the models here, wasting everyone's time."

Tyler shrugged. "I had to do what I had to do."

April glanced at me, noting that I was frozen in place but trembling. "Well, it's obvious that she doesn't want to talk to you. I think you've done enough."

"Speak for yourself, honey," Gabe interjected. "He can disrespect me all he wants, whenever he wants," Gabe said, admiring Tyler's incredible body.

"Shut up, Gabe!" April snapped. She turned her eyes back on Tyler, her expression stony. "Please leave, Tyler." April said coldly. "We need to finish this up."

Tyler didn't respond, and instead made his way toward the judges' table. By this time, my heart was pounding and I could hardly breathe.

"Victoria," Tyler pleaded. "Please talk to me. I can explain what happened that night you walked in on me and Candice. If you let me." He reached out his hand to me when I didn't respond. "Come on," he urged, nodding toward the exit. "We can go out into the waiting room and talk."

I stared at his hand like it was poisonous, dueling emotions roiling through my body like a tidal wave.

"Tyler, don't make me have to call security," April commanded.

Tyler ignored her, pleading with those beautiful eyes of his. "Please, Victoria. All I'm asking for is a chance to tell you the truth."

"Oh, to hell with this," Gabe chipped in. "Vicky, you best take your cute little ass out there and hear him out! The man is making a fool of himself just to talk to you."

Gabe's words had a slight effect on me as I stared into Tyler's handsome face.

Maybe I should hear him out. I mean, Gabe might be right. Why would Tyler go through all this trouble to see me after all this time unless he cares for me?

I almost did it. I almost reached out and took his hand.

"I'm calling security," April growled, taking my silence as proof that I was mortified and didn't want to talk to him.

"Don't!" I jumped to my feet, grabbed my water bottle and dashed the rest of the contents into Tyler's face. "Go fuck

184

yourself!" I yelled.

Then I turned and ran from the room sobbing.

Tyler

Shit. That didn't go so well.

I wiped the water out of my eyes, feeling some of it drip down my neck, down my chest and beyond as the judges whispered amongst each other, casting glances my way.

April looked taken aback by Victoria's sudden burst of anger, frozen for several moments. Then she stood up and rose on her tip toes to look over my shoulder. "Thank you all for coming," she said loudly. "I'm very sorry about the unexpected disruption. For those of you who are interested, we will resume at noon tomorrow. Ashley will show you out."

The last remaining models were quickly ushered out by a young woman who looked like a model herself.

"You guys can leave as well," April said to her fellow judges. "I'll keep the votes and notes and hand them over to Christine when she comes back."

After several furtive whispers, the other judges, except for Gabe, got up and began walking out.

April turned on me when they were gone, her eyes furious. "What the hell was that?" she demanded. "All you're going to do is get Vicky into trouble with a stunt like that."

I shrugged. "That wasn't my intention. I just need five minutes with her. Five minutes."

April scowled. "And that makes it right?" she growled.

"You need to go and never come—" She paused and stared at me suspiciously. "Wait a minute. How did you know that Victoria would even be here? She doesn't usually work the judging panel."

I gave her a crooked grin. "I have my ways."

"Ugh!" April snarled. "You are so infuriating! I see why Victoria would get so pissed off when talking about you." April placed her hands on her hips. "Look, it's obvious your little stunt didn't work. So you'd better just head on out. I don't know what Christine will do about this, but I hope she puts your nuts in a vice. You need to be taught a lesson."

I shook my head. "I'm not leaving until I talk to her. At this point, I don't care what happens."

"I was hoping I wouldn't have to do this," April sighed. She made a flipping motion with her hand. "Gabe, please get security."

Gabe looked reluctant. "Why don't we just . . ."

"Gabe!" April cracked. "Now!"

"Alright!" whined Gabe, slowly getting up. "Don't get your panties all in a bunch."

He made it couple of steps before I said sternly, "Wait."

Gabe paused, turning around to regard me, his eyebrow raised.

"Hear me out," I said to April. "Just let me tell *you* my side of the story and I'll leave."

April pursed her lips, undecided.

"Five minutes," I urged. "I just want Victoria to know that I . . ." A lump appeared in my throat, making it difficult to speak. "That I love her," I finally managed. It was hard to say it.

I'd been thinking it for a long time, but my words were carefully chosen. I knew it would give April pause.

Shock etched across April's face at my announcement, exactly what I was hoping for. Even I was surprised by it. It felt very strange to have those words come out of my mouth, especially after I'd sworn to never fall in love with a girl again.

"Wow," April gulped. "I was almost convinced. But not quite."

"Go on," Gabe persuaded. "That can't be all?"

"Gee, thanks for your support," I muttered.

Gabe winked.

"Promise me that if I don't like what you have to say, you'll put an end to this and never bother Victoria again."

I grinned. "Promise."

April stared at me suspiciously for a long time before letting out a huge sigh. "Fine, but make it quick."

Chapter 26
Victoria

How dare he show up like that? I thought, standing before the large window of Christine's office with my arms crossed and looking out at the darkening skyline.

After I'd run from the auditioning room, crying my eyes out, I made it back to the top floor, locking myself in Christine's office. There I felt safe, away from everyone. I'd gotten myself together and resumed my duties, working to try to forget what happened.

Still, there'd been a part of me that wanted to run back down and confront Tyler just as fast as I'd run out, to call him the scum of the earth, a lying bastard. It took all of my discipline, repeating an empowering litany over and over in my head, to stay put.

No, I was better off without him in my life.

A knock on the wall jolted me back from thought. "Hey Miss Boss Lady!"

April walked into the office, a concerned look on her face.

"Hey," I replied. I hadn't seen April since I ran from the auditioning room, and I wondered if she was mad at me. "How'd everything go?"

April walked over and set some papers down on Christine's desk and sighed. "Awful. I had to call off the rest of the audition. It's being rescheduled for tomorrow. I've already called Christine and confirmed. She was angry about it, but I think she has too much on her plate right now to worry about it. That is, as long as everything gets taken care of tomorrow."

April twisted one of her side ponytails around her index finger, looking thoughtful. "Something about Patty White is giving her an ulcer."

I know all about it, I thought.

"What about Tyler?" I asked. I hated how eager I sounded.

April stopped fooling with her hair and looked at me. "I sent him away."

"Did you have to call security?" For some reason that was important to me. I liked the idea of Tyler fighting with security guards and getting thrown out on his ass. It would show his cocky ass right.

April shook her head. "No, he left on his own."

"Oh." I sounded so disappointed.

April walked over to stand next to me and placed a hand on my shoulder, looking me directly in the eyes. "Are you okay?" she asked with concern.

For a moment, I thought about lying, but then I thought better of it. Since my ordeal with Tyler, April had been a great friend. She only wanted what was best for me.

"At first I wasn't," I replied. "I cried and cried, but then I slowly pulled it together." I sniffed. "Someone had to do the work around here."

"That's good," April said softly. "But I have a question."

"Huh?"

"Did you ever give Tyler a chance to explain why that girl was there that day?"

I scowled. "No, why should I? The skank was holding his dick while he was half-naked. What is there to explain? That she wasn't real? That I was having delusions? Please, April." I thought it was odd that April, who'd been the very one condemning Tyler, was asking if I'd given him a chance to explain his lies to me.

April studied me, understanding in her eyes. "Sometimes, Vicky, things aren't what they seem."

I glowered. "What the hell is that supposed to mean?"

Instead of answering, April turned toward the window. "It sure is a beautiful view at dusk," she murmured appreciatively.

Doesn't beat the view from Tyler's office, I thought.

"It is," I admitted, wondering what April's deal was. "A beautiful view and an ugly day."

"It wasn't that bad."

Are you kidding me?

I turned away and walked over to Christine's desk, ready to go home. April was suddenly acting too weird for me. "It's time to get out of here." I paused, looking around the desk to make sure Christine's things were exactly how she liked them.

"Hey, April."

"What's up?"

"Can you tell Gabe to bring Christine's *White Book* before you go? He came by here a bit ago, asking to borrow it. I want everything to be where it's supposed to be when Christine gets here. She'll have a fit if it isn't here in the morning," I said.

April turned to regard me, a twinkle in her eye. "Sure. I'll send him up as soon as I track him down." She walked toward the office doorway but stopped to ask, "Do you need anything?"

Okay, now I really know she's acting weird.

I crossed my arms. "No. Just that book. Now," I said with my best Christine impression.

April saluted me with a laugh. "Right on it, Boss."

I gagged. "Gross."

Leaving a peal of laughter in her wake, April left the office, practically skipping out.

"Weirdo," I muttered when she was gone.

While killing time for Gabe, I went about tidying up Christine's office, making sure nothing was out of place. Christine was a neat freak, and if she came back with so much as a pen out of place, I was sure I'd never hear the end of it.

I still couldn't believe that she'd let me run her office for a day. Me, the girl she'd practically tortured since coming to work for her. Me, the girl who thought she was doomed to be a slave for Christine for most of her adult life, only to be tossed to the wayside when she wasn't needed.

But things were beginning to change. Christine started treating me with at least a hint of respect, and she obviously had enough faith in me to give me this opportunity.

All in all, I thought I did a good job if not for the disaster in the audition room, even if I was practically an answering machine.

"C'mon, Gabe, where are you?" I muttered, glancing at Christine's antique clock on the wall. I was already here later than normal. The sun had sunk behind the horizon, leaving a darkened skyline twinkling with lights.

Sighing in frustration, I sat down at Christine's desk and called Gabe's extension. I didn't know why he was taking so damn long. He worked several floors below me, but he still should've been burning wheels to get that book back to me. He was usually the first one out the door every day.

The phone rang several times before his answering machine picked up. "This is Gabriel, your fashion divanista. I'll get back to you guys whenever I feel like it . . . BITCHES!"

Beep.

I swear to God, he only had that message somehow specifically for me. There's no way he'd survived working for Christine that long with a voicemail like that. "Gabe, what the hell are you doing?" I demanded. "I'm ready to go home. Why aren't you here yet? You know who's going to be killed when Christine comes back in tomorrow morning looking for . . ."

"This?" asked a deep voice at the doorway.

I looked up and my heart jumped in my chest.

Tyler.

Again.

He was standing in the doorway, this time with clothes on, a tux, no less, holding Christine's *White Book* in his hands. Five o'clock shadow shaded his jaw as he grinned at me with his enigmatic eyes.

I swear on my life, he never looked more hot and sexy than in that moment. *What the hell did he do between now and the last time I saw him?* I wondered, awed that he would show up looking so formal just for me.

"What—" I began.

"Am I doing here?" Tyler finished for me.

It felt like the cat had my tongue. I nodded.

"I've come to see you, what else?" He said, as if it was plainly obvious. "And to bring you this book." Keeping his eyes on me, he swaggered over to Christine's desk and set the book down before me.

April must have known about this . . . that's why she was acting so differently.

"At your service, Madame," Tyler said dutifully, treating me to a majestic bow. His charm was powerful; it always had been.

Don't fall for his antics and let him prey on your emotions, that annoying voice urged. *Get him out of here.*

Gathering all the mental strength that I had at my command, I shot to my feet, stabbing a finger at the door. "Get out!" I shouted. Though I tried to sound as threatening as possible, I actually sounded frightened.

Tyler didn't budge, his eyes still twinkling, unfazed by my barely-there wrath. "You sure about that?"

"I'm positive!" I hissed, trembling all over. "You're a cheating scumbag and you don't deserve me!"

Tyler's grin evaporated and he looked at me with surprising anger. "I never cheated on you," he growled. "I swear on my life."

"You may not have, because I happened to catch you, but you were about to!"

"What you saw was one moment," Tyler said calmly. "You have no idea what happened before that."

Why am I even listening to this? I wondered.

"Will you calm down and let me explain without freaking out?" Tyler pleaded, a gentle tone in his voice that made me feel like mush inside. "I promise you'll understand better once I'm done. And if you still don't want to talk to me when it's over, I'll leave and you'll never have to hear from me again."

For some reason, the thought of never hearing from him again really bothered me, even though I'd spent the last several months avoiding him at all costs.

Maybe I should just listen, I thought, *if only to see how ridiculous his lie is going to be.*

I bit my lower lip, deep in thought while Tyler gazed at me with an earnestness that I found surprising.

Screw it. Just give him a chance to explain himself and be done with it.

"Go ahead then," I said finally, crossing my arms across my chest and sticking my nose up at the ceiling in a snobby manner. "For all the good it will do you."

Tyler let out a relieved sigh. "Thank you, Vicky."

It was the first time he'd called me *Vicky*. I had to admit, it sounded good to my ears.

Then he began telling me about what happened after I left him. How his ex-girlfriend suddenly showed up and demanded re-entry to his life and how she'd forced herself on him after he demanded that she leave.

"And you walked into the room right as she grabbed me," Tyler said as he finished his tale. "I was about to forcefully remove her, but then I thought better of it. I didn't want her to accuse me of something, she's the biggest gold digger I've ever known, after all. I was in thought about how to handle the

194

situation, and she took advantage of it. That's the God's honest truth."

I stood there for a long while, mulling Tyler's story over in my head. For all my suspicion about his being a player, his story sure sounded genuine. His tone sounded genuine. Not one word he said sounded like a lie. But then again, that's what he was known for, a honey tongue.

"And she's the one who caused me to lose my faith in relationships to begin with," Tyler continued. "Trust me when I say that I'd never allow her in my life again. I tell you now, I've never been hurt by much of anything, even when my parents divorced. But what she did . . ." He shook his head, his eyes haunted. "It fucking destroyed me, probably because I'd allowed myself to grow such a huge ego that I never thought something like that would happen to me. I gave her everything . . . all of me . . . and still it wasn't enough. I know what it feels like to be cheated on, and I would never do that to you."

It was hardly fathomable to me. What kind of girl would cheat on Tyler Locklin? He had everything. I mean, he was young, good looking, rich.

And he's good in bed, said the voice in my head.

"So when you hear about me being a player, it was all because I was acting out my pain. I'm quite certain none of those girls ever had any inclination that I was interested in them beyond that first night. In a way, I was protecting myself. I'd put a barrier up, and I refused to let anyone get through it. That is, until you came along."

I could tell it was difficult for him to get the words out. I'd never seen him so conflicted by his emotions before . . . and I liked it. It was nice knowing that he was capable of it.

"What about that crap about my lips when I was getting your measurements? I started out no different than any of the other girls you've discarded," I demanded.

Tyler cleared his throat, feigning embarrassment. "That was just me being me. Besides, it was before I knew you." He chuckled at me, winking. "But I gotta' say, I was absolutely right."

"Asshole!"

"Relax, I'm just kidding. Kind of."

I scowled. "Not funny. Not funny at all."

"Yeah it is, you just don't want to admit." He turned serious. "Do you believe me?"

For once that voice in my mind was silent, a good sign.

"Maybe," I said coyly. "But what happened to your ex? Am I just supposed to believe she left and never came back?"

"She did come back," Tyler admitted.

I tensed up, feeling anger rise up in my throat.

"But she left when she got what she wanted," Tyler added quickly, seeing my dark scowl.

"Which was?"

"Money."

"Are you serious?" I demanded.

Tyler looked helpless. "It was a quick fix, I admit. I had enough shit going on, and I just wanted the problem to go away. She'll probably be back, but we can cross that bridge when we get there."

A ping of sympathy went through me, seeing the earnestness in his eyes, the pain. He really was telling the truth.

"I believe you," I said, not bothering to ask how much he'd had to pay her to go away. I suppose it really didn't matter, and I figured the number would piss me off and we'd be back at square one.

Tyler let out an audible sigh, his expression one of relief.

"But that doesn't mean I'm just ready to start right back where we left off," I was quick to add.

It would take some time to adjust to the idea that we were back on again, especially spending the last few months hating him.

I have to make him suffer a little, I thought. *I went through a lot of mental anguish during the time I was avoiding him . . . even if some of it was my fault for not giving him the time of day to explain what actually happened.*

"Of course," Tyler said diplomatically. "I wouldn't expect you to be."

Uh huh.

I glowered at how he was agreeing with anything I said. I thought I'd test him, see if he was even listening to what I was saying. "And I want five hundred thousand dollars."

Of course I wasn't serious about the proposition. *I just want to hear him disagree with me on **something**.*

Tyler didn't blink. "You got it."

I laughed, knowing he was lying through his teeth. "Don't push it, buddy." I glanced at the clock. It was a quarter past the hour. We needed to leave, but I still had a few things I wanted to say to him.

I shook my head. "I just can't believe that you went through all this . . . just for me."

197

"I can," Tyler said softly. He paused, like he was pondering if he should say his next words. "I love you."

His words hit me like a gunshot to the stomach. "What?" I asked breathlessly. I must've been imagining things. I'd hoped to hear those words, but I thought they'd never come.

Tyler walked around to my side of the desk, moved Christine's chair out of the way, and turned me to face him. "I love you," he repeated in a soft, sexy growl while cupping my right cheek in his hand and gently stroking it. "I've known it for a long time now."

Lost in the conviction of his beautiful blue eyes, I could hardly breathe. Love me? Tyler Locklin? I searched his face for deceit or some clue that he could be lying to me, but I couldn't even find a hint of it.

He loved me. Tyler Locklin loved me.

"Don't cry," Tyler soothed, taking his thumb and wiping the tear that slid down the side of my face.

"I love you too," I breathed in his face before kissing him hard on the lips.

His powerful arms wrapped around me and he bent me back into Christine's desk as our tongues found each other's.

"Stop!" I gasped a moment later, pushing him back and straightening. The fires were raging. Another moment and I would've lost myself.

Tyler grinned at me, that mischievous, boyish grin. "Stop? I was just getting started." He pulled me into him and I could feel his big, hard cock pressing up against my stomach, ready to go.

"Uh," I moaned as Tyler ran his hands up my thighs and

around my hips to grab and squeeze my ass. "What are you doing?"

"What do you think?" Tyler replied, his breath scorching my cheek as he brushed his lips against it.

By this time, I was burning up from the close proximity of his body, feeling absolutely breathless, my limbs trembling all over. I could feel sweat gathering on various parts of my body.

It's like ninety degrees in here! Damn, I'm in hell!

"Wait!" I protested weakly. "This is Christine's office!"

Tyler laughed, uncaring. "So?" He delivered a strong kiss to my lips.

"So . . ." I gasped, "we . . . just . . . can't."

Tyler kissed me again. "We can't?"

"N . . . no," I managed. "We can't."

Tyler squeezed my right butt cheek. "Who says that we can't?"

"Me. Christine." My protests were so weak. Even I didn't believe them. "She'll kill me."

"Well, you should know by now, I'm not too big on following the rules," Tyler growled, his lips finding my neck, raising my temperature up another notch. "No reason to start obeying them now."

My defenses crumbled like a piece of paper at the intensity in his words. Who was I kidding? Every inch of Tyler Locklin was . . . addicting.

Smothering my neck, he placed his hands under my ass and lifted me up onto the desk, pushing my torso back onto it and knocking all of the items on Christine's desk to the floor.

I'm dead, I thought, briefly worried about the mess we

were making.

My worries quickly vanished as Tyler bent down and continued kissing me, his hands roving all over my body with expert deftness. I moaned with pleasure and ran my fingers through his hair, filled with an almost giddy excitement.

My pent up sexual frustration and the risky naughtiness of it all made it that much more exciting, adding an edge to our passion.

I pulled on Tyler's hair as he bit into my blouse with his teeth, and with a feral jerk, he ripped it open, displaying my bra and quavering belly.

I looked up at him, awed at the primal lust on display. He was beautiful in all his horny glory, a beast that had come to have his way with his prey.

He practically tore off my bra, exposing my breasts, feasting on them like he was starving. I ran my hand down his back, feeling the incredible muscles beneath his suit, reveling in his hunger for my body.

I gasped when his lips wrapped around an erect nipple, his free hand reaching down beneath my skirt and rubbing me through my now soaked panties.

"Ohh," I groaned, holding onto his hair tightly, enjoying the feel of him sucking on my nipples and massaging me at the same time.

My nipples proved not enough to sate his incredible hunger, as he drifted down to my waist and quickly removed my skirt and panties in one swift motion.

I cried out once again when his mouth completely covered my pussy and he began his feast. Looking up at me with those intense eyes of his, he held onto my thighs as I squirmed all over Christine's desk.

"Fuck!" I cried, squirming, sprawling my arms out behind me, knocking the last bit of items off the desk. I was bucking like a wild animal, but I was no match for Tyler's strength. He held my lower body in place, his lips stuck to me like glue. "Oh my God!"

Two fingers slipped inside me slowly, my stomach clamping down in response to his furious assault. My breathing quickened, and a thunderstorm was brewing inside my belly, ready to unleash its fury.

My toes curled up and my eyes rolled back inside my head as Tyler continued his onslaught, flicking his tongue up and down on my clit. "Shit!" I cried, grabbing a handful of his hair and clinging on for dear life. "I'm coming!"

Emboldened, the bastard went in harder, faster, giving me all his powerful jaws could muster until I could hold on no longer.

I blacked out momentarily. My own cries were the first thing I heard a moment later as I convulsed all over his face. He continued to hold my lower body in place, his whole mouth still clamped down on me, taking all of me in.

After the last tremor ran through my thighs, he finally let me go and stood up.

"That was intense," I said weakly, sweat covering my forehead. "I'd forgotten how skilled you were with that mouth of yours."

Tyler grinned at me, wiping his face with the back of his hand. "That I am." A huge bulge was pressing against his black pants, a sign that he wasn't done with me. "But I'm only just getting started." He took off his blazer and then swiftly unbuttoned his dress shirt and flared it open, showing off his fabulous six pack. On impulse, I ran my fingers along the hard lines of his abs, marveling at how well-defined they were.

Sometimes I thought Tyler's body had been sculpted by God himself, it was so exquisite. He grinned at me, loving every minute of my admiration of his body.

He pulled back, dropping his pants around his ankles, his big cock bouncing out and up and down. I yearned to slide down to my knees and take him in my mouth, but I knew Tyler had other plans for me.

"Are you ready?" he asked me, looking me in the eyes.

I wasn't sure why he was asking. Of course I was ready. I wanted him to fuck me like no tomorrow.

"Of course I am," I replied. "What're you waiting for?"

Grinning, Tyler bent down to plant a kiss on my cheek. "That's my girl," he whispered in my ear.

He penetrated me fully in one deep thrust, his cock going to the hilt inside my canal.

I gasped.

Grabbing my breasts and squeezing them firmly, he began to slowly thrust in and out of me.

I can't believe this, I thought. *I'm getting fucked by Tyler Locklin in Christine's office.*

The thought faded away as Tyler thrust deeply once again, the friction of our bodies against the desk filling the room with sounds of creaking wood and the clap of flesh.

He pushed my legs back almost to my head, and I was

thankful that I was pretty flexible. He leaned forward into me, breathing hard in my face and delivering passionate pecks to my lips every time he thrusted inward.

"Are you ready?" he asked me between thrusts, staring me deep in the eyes, his breathing labored, sweat beading down his forehead and dripping onto me.

I hesitated for a moment, then nodded. I was suddenly overcome with a range of emotions as his cock slid in and out of me. Pleasure. Pain. Happiness. Euphoria.

"Yes!" I choked, staring directly into his eyes and seeing only love reflected there. "I'm ready. I've been ready. Show me what I've been missing."

Tyler nodded at me, and that mischievous grin I knew so well formed on his face. He released my legs, pulling me up against him, but making sure his cock didn't slip out of me. "I've longed for this feeling once again," he whispered. His thrusts became slower. Harder. Fuller. I ran my fingers up and down his back, and settled them on his firm ass, guiding him into me and encouraging him.

"Fuck me," I whispered sweetly, eager to feel him explode inside me.

That did the trick.

After one last powerful thrust, he threw back his head. "Ohh fuck!" He cried.

I dug my nails into his back at the same time, coming hard with him in that perfect moment. He collapsed down onto me, our sweat mingling with each other as our bodies shook against each other from pleasure.

A deep sigh escaped his lips after the last twitch of his

cock. He pulled himself up and fell back onto the desk beside me, exhausted. The sound of our ragged breathing filled our ears and I smiled contentedly.

We'd done something so naughty, but something so beautiful at the same time.

After a few moments, Tyler raised up, pulling me in close to kiss my forehead. "I love you," he said, looking into my eyes with that same deep love that so touched my heart.

I knew then that whatever happened from here on out, Tyler would always be there for me.

No matter what.

I smiled at him, my heart soaring. "I love you too."

Charles

I tapped my fingers against my desk impatiently, resisting the urge to curse again. My contact told me he had something for me. Problem was, I hadn't heard from the bastard since, and he was supposed to have been here half an hour ago.

"Where the hell is he?" I muttered, glancing at my watch. It was closing hours for Armex. Most people would be gone home by now, but not everyone was required to be out. Not if they had important work to do.

And there's nothing more important than what I'm doing, I thought darkly. *Sealing my position within this company before it's too late.*

Tyler Locklin was a woman-chasing, incompetent fool.

And the sooner he was brought down, the better.

He's a disgrace, and I'm going to make sure that he's widely recognized as the talentless scoundrel that he is.

After sitting for another ten minutes, I grabbed my mobile phone and slid my finger over the lock screen. If my contact had lied, he'd be sorry.

Before I could begin to dial a certain number, the door to my office opened gently and in walked the man I was waiting on.

"Finally," I growled. "You took forever. I was beginning to think you had second thoughts. Did you bring what we discussed?"

Though his hood was pulled low, even I could see the grin that touched his jaw line.

He walked over and tossed a large envelope on my desk. Eagerly, I snatched up the package and pushed another, fatter, envelope across the desk to him.

"You have my thanks," I practically drooled. "When I hired you, I never thought you'd get something this good. You're worth every penny."

My contact grabbed the envelope and weighed it in his hand before sticking it into the folds his hoodie. "You know what you're going to do with those?" he asked.

I bit back a sarcastic reply. He's good, but I didn't pay him to be nosy. But what did it matter? In a day or two, I would have what I want. Tyler Locklin would be ruined.

For good.

I couldn't keep a nefarious grin off my face as I replied, "Get rid of a thorn in my side, once and for all."

Chapter 27
Tyler

"I'm so proud of you, son," my father said while I was sitting in his office after a long day at work. It'd been a week after Victoria and I had gotten back together and I'd never been happier. "You made such a change in a short period of time."

After getting back together, I'd thrown myself into my duties with renewed vigor, trying to fix all the problems that so worried my father.

If he needed me for a specific task, I was there. If he wanted something done that required my expertise, I did it instead of passing it off to a lackey.

I wasn't sure what had me so motivated, but I had my guess.

With Victoria by my side, I was a changed man. Through and through. "Ah, thanks, Dad," I said.

He shook his head. "That was one helluva presentation you gave this afternoon. I haven't seen you that excited in years."

"Did you like it? I must admit, I can't take all the credit. Jeff helped me for hours getting prepared."

"Even still, you have such a way with words. A charm about you that I respect. You could definitely be a public speaker."

"Please, Dad," I muttered. "I hate speaking in front of

groups. I'm dreading this thing I have to do at Brad's wedding as it is."

Dad grinned. "Ah, Brad. How is that fella nowadays?"

"He's hanging in there," I replied. "Once the wedding is over I'm sure he'll be better."

Dad looked emphatic. "The poor bastard."

Suddenly, the doors to the office burst open. Startled, I jumped to my feet, as did my dad.

"Hello, gentlemen," Charles Whitmore greeted us cheerily, strolling into the room as if he owned the place.

He made a waving motion at us. "Please, please. Have a seat. Don't you both stand up on my account."

Father slowly sank back into his chair, but I remained standing. I knew by the smug sound of Charles's voice that the bastard had something up his sleeve.

"What the hell are you doing barging in here without knocking, Charles?" Father demanded. "I was having a private conversation with my son."

Charles walked over to his desk, sparing a quick glance my way. "Oh yes, your son."

My dad scowled in annoyance "Yes, my son. You do remember Tyler, don't you?"

Charles laughed. "Of course I do. Who couldn't remember the cocky asshole that's caused Armex major problems and robbed me of my rightful position?"

The only thing keeping me from turning Charles's face inside out was knowing that I'd probably spend a night in jail and would be sued for millions of dollars. Still, it'd almost be worth it.

Dad froze, staring at Charles suspiciously. "Show some respect, Charles. I'm not going tell you again."

Charles's face twisted into a mask of fury. "What I remember, Mr. Locklin, is being promised a promotion."

"So that's what this is all about," Dad muttered, his eyes glued to Charles's annoying mug. "You're still upset over all that."

"You're damn right I'm upset, sir!"

"I suggest you get over it. You're an asset, so I'm going to cut you some slack, but you're pushing it."

Charles grew silent and stood there fuming. I watched him closely, wondering if I was going to have to drag him out of the office if he refused to leave. I'd enjoy manhandling the little prick immensely.

"Fine," Charles snarled finally. "I didn't want have to do this, but you leave me no choice." Keeping his eyes on my dad, he stuck his hand inside his blazer, reaching for something.

My eyes went wide and I was gripped by panic as Charles grabbed something.

I guess I'd been watching too many movies, but my heart was suddenly in my throat, and I quickly leaped across the space separating us. A second later, I collided into Charles with a grunt, knocking him to the floor and sending the folder in his hand flying.

"What the hell? Get off of me!" Charles yelled, struggling to push me off.

Scattered across the floor, I saw pictures, scores of them. My dad was already picking one up. "What the hell is this?" he demanded.

I got a glimpse of one of the photos, and immediately a feeling of dread twisted in my stomach.

In the photo you could see Victoria and me, her legs pushed back to her head, and the back of my masculine figure as I pounded away.

Anger threatened to overwhelm me, and it was all I could do to keep from going over and choking the worthless life out of Charles.

"That," Charles said smugly, rising to his feet and dusting himself off, a look of sick pleasure coming over his face, "is your son fucking his stepsister."

My father looked at me with question. The look I returned him told him all he needed to know.

"Looks like Tyler" he muttered. "But I don't see his face."

"Keep looking, you'll find it in there somewhere," Charles purred. "Now that we know the situation here—let's discuss my promotion. Or these are going straight to the media."

"You son of a bitch!" I yelled, going for Charles. Dad grabbed me before I took a few steps and pulled me back.

Charles grinned at me with that smug look of his, pissing me off further. "So you see, James, your son is nothing but a liability to this company like everyone has known all along. I'm not asking for anything that isn't warranted here. Tyler will forever be a thorn in Armex's backside while he remains employed here."

Dad looked around at all the photos scattered around his office, gathering his thoughts. "So let me get this straight. You want me to get rid of my son in exchange for your not releasing these photos to the press?"

Charles beamed. "Correct."

"Charles, I'm not the sort of man that responds well to blackmail." Dad snorted and turned toward me. In his eyes, I could see the anger reflected there. After all the great work I'd been doing lately, I'd now managed to upset him again.

"I'm sorry—" I began.

My dad waved me off. "Don't be." He turned back to Charles, who was smugly adjusting his clothing, looking as if he knew that my title, what he'd been after for so long, was finally his. "These photographs are truly unfortunate," Dad said. "And I can't tell you how upset I am that my son is a part of them."

"Don't worry," Charles said, casting a triumphant glance my way. "No one will ever see them, and maybe Tyler will learn to have better judgement in the future—"

"But I won't be meeting your demands," Dad interrupted.

Charles froze. "What?"

What the hell are you doing? I wondered.

"You heard me," my father growled, tossing the photograph he'd had in his hand to the floor with the rest of them.

"You're making a very big mistake," Charles warned.

"In fact," my father retorted, unperturbed. "Once my lawyers are done with you, you're going to be lucky if you avoid jail time."

Despite the dire situation, I let out a mocking chuckle. At least he had my back.

Charles shook his head in disbelief. "You'd throw your

company's image down the drain all on the account of your son? Someone who disrespects the position he holds?"

"Our competitors will use it against us, no doubt. But we'll recover," Dad said, walking around to his desk and placing both hands on either side, fixing Charles with a glare that looked as if it could burn a whole right through him. "But you? You won't recover."

Charles was at a loss for words, his mouth opening and closing like a fish.

"Now you can take your threats and shove them up your ass, because you're fired." He said, making Donald Trump sound like an amateur. "Get him out of here."

"My pleasure." I grinned.

Though I was worried about what would happen with Armex and the effect on my relationship with Victoria if the pictures were released, it was comforting to know that my dad had my back.

I walked over and grabbed Charles by the arm. "Let's go."

"You can't fire me!" Charles yelled as I led him to do the door. "This place will crumble without me!"

Dad laughed. "Everyone is replaceable. Someday you'll learn that, Charles."

Charles struggled against my grip as I dragged him, but he was no match for my strength. I dragged him, kicking and screaming like the little bitch that he was, out of the office.

I walked over and gathered all the damning photos and stuck them back in the envelope and turned to face my father. "So," I said. "What now?"

I expected him to go off on me, yell at me and shame me for putting us into this position. Instead he grinned at me and said, "It looks like we're hiring."

Chapter 28
Victoria

"I heard you had quite a week," Christine said to me as I stood before her desk. My boss was sitting there looking super sharp as usual in her leopard dress of all things, flawless makeup and an elegant updo, smiling at me as if I were the winner of some unknown prize.

Christine had continued to progressively show me more respect. She was even asking for my opinion on matters and complimenting me on what I wore, which was an absolute rarity.

All in all, I had to wonder if finally standing up to her that day I almost quit caused her to respect me.

"Yes, ma'am," I replied respectfully.

She sat back in her seat, her eyes on me. "I heard that Tyler Locklin interrupted one of my auditions."

I paused, not sure where this was going. Christine had known about this incident since the day it happened, but she was just now mentioning it. I hadn't told her that I'd resumed my relationship with Tyler, not sure how'd she react—not that it was any of her business. "Yeah, but the audition was almost over when he did, and April got rid of him fairly quickly. I'm sorry, Christine, I know I said he wouldn't cause any more trouble."

Christine raised a skeptical eyebrow. "Did she?"

"Yeah."

"Then what was he doing up here in my office after

hours?"

I froze. Did she know? There's no way she could've known, could she?

"One of the interns said she saw him coming up here."

Relief flowed through me as I realized Christine didn't know the extent of what went on in her office. I'd done my best to clean up and get everything exactly right, after all.

"He came up with some ruse to get his way up here. We had a little talk . . . and worked things out."

"You did?" Christine asked in surprise. "Well, good for you. Don't put up with any shit from him though."

"Yes, ma'am."

"Okay, enough with the chit-chatting, Victoria. Get to work," she said. "I'm expecting a call from Pierre about scheduling a meeting."

"Yes, Mrs. Finnerman." I turned and began to walk from the office.

"Oh and, Victoria?" Christine called.

I paused, half-turning to regard her. "Yes?"

Christine had a serene smile on her face. "I could use some coffee."

* * *

"Open your eyes," Tyler commanded, removing the blindfold from around my head. He'd come and picked me up after work, a tradition we'd started before our little split. He told me had something to show me, but he would only take me if I agreed to put on a blindfold.

Suspicious, it took some convincing for him to get me to agree, but of course I eventually gave in. Tyler always gets what he wants. Besides, I've always loved surprises.

Anxious, I popped open my eyes. It was an empty building. "What is this, and why are we here?" I asked, confused.

"It's yours. You're standing in your new startup location," Tyler said. "Sure, it needs some work, but we'll have it whipped up in no time."

"Oh my God," I said, tears pooling in my eyes. "It's amazing!" I managed before frowning. "But I had the impression you weren't serious about this."

Tyler waved me off. "Nonsense. I admit, I did suggest it a little too quickly before, but I've consulted with a few experts, and we're going to make this work." He grinned at me.

Tears came to my eyes and I felt weak in my knees. "I can't believe this," I said, noticing that little smirk he had on his face. "What? You have that *and that's not all* look going on right now."

"It's the best part. Christine Finnerman has agreed to send over her two best lieutenants to work alongside you."

"April and Gabe," I breathed, feeling dizzy. This had to be some sort of dream.

"I-I-I-" I stuttered, unable to find the words.

"Love me?" Tyler finished.

"Yes, of course that, but . . . what if this business fails? What if I fail? And do I even want to know what it took to get Christine to agree to that?"

"Then it fails and at least you tried. This is your dream, and it's right in front of you. It's time for you to go out and seize it. But I know you three aren't going to fail," Tyler said firmly. "All that slaving for Christine is going to pay off, trust me."

215

"You didn't answer my last question."

"Details, details. Does it really matter?" Tyler said with a grin.

I don't think I loved Tyler more than I did in that moment. I stood on my tiptoes and gave him a deep kiss.

"Damn, I should give you surprises like this more often," Tyler breathed when I finally pulled back away from him, breathless.

I giggled. "Oh shut it."

"Seriously, I want more of where that came from."

I playfully poked him in the stomach. "Later."

"Promise?"

"Promise.

Tyler stared at me wearily. "All right. I'm going to hold you to that."

I smiled, then sighed a second later.

"What's the matter now?" Tyler asked.

"I just don't know how I'm ever going to repay you for all of this."

Suddenly, Tyler's face brightened. "I know exactly how you can repay me."

I stared at him warily. "What is it?"

"You can be my date to Brad's wedding tomorrow."

"Ugh," I groaned. "I don't know. I don't really have anything to wear."

Tyler pulled me in close, the smell of his cologne that I so loved tickling my nose. "You're in fashion. I'm sure you can find something. And it's not a request," he added. "It's an order."

Epilogue
Tyler

There's a saying that you get what you pay for, and I got exactly that with Brad's wedding. The event was a lavish affair, being held at the Promade. It was a small fortune to rent it for the day, but it was worth it.

All the wedding guests were dressed in the high-end attire designed by Christine. I'd supplied the money for top-notch catering, a band, and best of all, relieved my best friend of tremendous stress.

Not to say that he wasn't still stressed. Even with everything I'd done to help, Brad still couldn't help being nervous. It was his wedding, after all.

"Calm down, man," I whispered to him as we waited. We were both dressed in almost identical tuxes, black and white, our shoes freshly shined and our hair nicely styled.

"You're going to stroke out before Katie even makes her way down the aisle."

"I just want everything perfect for her," Brad replied, and I could understand.

All the guests were waiting. The music was about to start and I was about to walk with Brad out to the altar.

"Get ahold of yourself," I growled. I felt like Brad was being ridiculous.

Before he could reply, a tiny dog, a Yorkshire Terrier

dressed in a tuxedo, came running to me.

"What the hell is this?" I demanded with a ridiculous laugh when the dog reached me, wondering what the hell a dog was doing here.

Brad eyed the dog and groaned. "That's Katie's little baby, Hercules. Fitting name for a five-pound dog, huh? She doesn't go anywhere without him. I told you she's an animal lover. Anyway, she insisted he be a part of the wedding. Sorry I didn't tell you, but don't worry, he's well-behaved."

I shook my head. "You'll never learn to put your foot down."

Brad grimaced. "That's not all. He's supposed to walk in with us."

I turned on him and rolled my eyes. "Hey, whatever floats your boat. It's your wedding."

"Let's go," I ordered. "It's time."

Brad pulled himself together, and when Katie reached the altar, he looked in total control of himself. I was proud of him.

The priest began, and I found my thoughts drifting to Victoria and what the future might hold for us. I could see her with the guests, and she looked absolutely stunning.

"And now you may kiss the bride!" The priest cried exultantly at the end.

With a smile on his face, Brad locked lips with Katie, and the crowd went wild, confetti flying everywhere. Hercules even got in on the excitement, running from person to person, looking for attention.

Victoria smiled at me while clapping, and I made my way

over to her, grabbing her hand. "I've never seen a best dog at a wedding before," she said as we made our way to the punch bowl.

I rolled my eyes. "He's cute, but don't even get me started on that one."

"I think I might want one just like him."

"That's going to take some serious convincing," I said with a grin.

Victoria laughed, her eyes sparkling. "I was just kidding. Kind of."

It was time for my speech. At first I was nervous as I got up onto the stage, not sure what I was going to say. I'd originally prepared a speech, but then I decided against it because I was usually good at talking off the top of my head. The words seemed to flow right through me and I found myself enjoying it, making light-hearted jokes about Brad and causing the audience to laugh.

"To Brad," I said as I came to the conclusion of my speech, raising my wine glass to toast the audience, "and his new wife."

The crowd went wild.

"That was a great speech," Victoria complimented, coming up and wrapping her arm around my waist. She smiled up at me, and my heart jumped in my chest at the sight of her. She looked so beautiful and so happy. I was proud that she was mine.

"Wasn't it?" I asked.

Victoria's eyes sparkled as she looked up at me. "So, um, I think I have a little surprise of my own."

I arched an eyebrow curiously. "Oh yeah? What's that?"

Victoria bit her lower lip in a teasing manner. "Well, you remember that deposit you made?"

I frowned in confusion. "Huh? What deposit?"

"The one you made after pounding me into submission," Victoria replied with a mischievous grin that I daresay rivaled one of my own.

"Oh," I said. "*That.*" I thought for a second before I grasped her meaning. "You mean I'm going to be . . ."

"A daddy," Victoria said in excitement.

She ran her fingers up my shoulders coyly. "Are you ready?"

Sweat beaded my forehead, and I actually felt dizzy for the first time that evening—and I hadn't even started drinking yet. Not from nervousness, but from the whirlwind of emotion now hitting me all at once.

"I am," I said, smiling, picking Victoria up into an almost bear hug and planting a deep, passionate kiss on her.

If you enjoyed this book, please take a moment to leave a review. As an independent author, I can use all the reviews I can get!

Made in the USA
Las Vegas, NV
20 February 2021